The Advanced RPG Guide to Becoming an Expert Dungeon Master

For Experienced Game Masters Who Seek Ultimate Expertise Over Their Craft

Eric Heim & Alexander Cosic

Copyright © 2022 Eric Heim & Alexander Cosic

All rights reserved.

The content contained within this book may not be reproduced, duplicated, or transmitted without direct written permission from the author or the publisher.

Under no circumstances will any blame or legal responsibility be held against the publisher, or author, for any damages, reparation, or monetary loss due to the information contained within this book, either directly or indirectly.

Legal Notice: This book is copyright protected. It is only for personal use. You cannot amend, distribute, sell, use, quote, or paraphrase any part, or the content within this book, without the consent of the author or publisher.

Disclaimer Notice: Please note the information contained within this document is for educational and entertainment purposes only. All effort has been executed to present accurate, up-to-date, reliable, and complete information. No warranties of any kind are declared or implied.

Readers acknowledge that the author is not engaged in the rendering of legal, financial, medical, or professional advice. The content within this book has been derived from various sources. Please consult a licensed professional before attempting any techniques outlined in this book.

By reading this document, the reader agrees that under no circumstances is the author responsible for any losses, direct or indirect, that are incurred as a result of the use of the information contained within this document, including, but not limited to, errors, omissions, or inaccuracies.

Ebook ISBN: 978-1-965673-06-5
Paperback ISBN: 978-1-965673-07-2
Hardcover ISBN: 978-1-965673-08-9

Table of Contents

Introduction 5

Chapter 1: A Worldbuilding & Homebrewing Crash Course 9

    Worldbuilding 101 11

    Creating a Sense of Space 16

    Campaign-Influenced World Evolution 19

    Homebrewing Your Own Fun 24

    Making Custom Characters for Your Players 55

    Steal Like a Thief - You Can Get Away with It 63

    Conclusion: The Edge of the Known World 67

Chapter 2: Creating Longer Campaigns 70

    Designing for Longevity 75

    Story-important NPCs 93

    Executing on a Good Design 104

    Conclusion: From Plot Hooks to Glory 111

Chapter 3: Campaign Management 114

    Adapting to Player Choices 115

    Managing the Ever-Evolving Complexity of the World and the Campaign 124

Managing Player Dynamics 129

Conclusion: The Aftermath of Mayhem 138

Chapter 4: Crafting a Great Session 140

Creating an Atmosphere: Setting the Scene 141

Balancing Prepared and Improvised Encounters . 162

Managing Combat Immersion 171

Mixing Up Encounters 174

Role-Playing Tips 180

Conclusion: Setting the Stage for Magic 184

Chapter 5: Growth 188

Player Communication 190

Becoming a Master Storyteller 228

Developing Your Own Unique Style 239

Conclusion: Beyond the Final Roll 241

Chapter 6: Ending 244

The Final Boss 245

Epilogue 250

How to Conclude an Entire Campaign 254

Is This the End? 256

Introduction

Beneath the deep indigo canopy of starlight, your adventurers gather around the crackling campfire, the air heavy with anticipation and the faint aroma of distant pine. At long last, they have found it - the ancient ruin of whispered lore, its tale carried on the lips of wanderers and cloaked in the shadows of countless forgotten nights. The stone doorway is before them, monumental and foreboding, its surface webbed with the scars of time and etched with cryptic runes that shimmer faintly in the moonlight.

The rogue steps forward, their breath anxiously drawn as curiosity sparkles within them. As you, the Dungeon Master, lean back with a knowing smile, your laughter about to roar like a distant thunderclap into the unknown. They think they are ready. They think their packs are full and their wits sharper than a blade. But *you* hold the cards of fate - twists that coil like smoke, surprises that linger just beyond the next turn, and a tapestry of plotlines eager to unfurl in the chaos.

This is the moment where simplicity fades, and the delicious complexity begins to weave its spell. The ruin is not just a relic of history but a stage for the extraordinary, where choices will clash, destinies entwine, and your adventurers discover that the truest magic lies not in the destination but in the labyrinth of the journey itself.

If you're a Dungeon Master because you hate feeling like a fish out of water, sorry, you're about to feel that way, but fear not - I'll teach you to walk on water and even swim on dry land by the time you're finished reading. Here is where you embark on the treacherous journey any magnificent worldbuilder, master storyteller, and maestro of rules must trek through.

Let me be clear: I do not doubt your qualifications as a DM. Whether you're a battle-hardened storyteller or fresh off learning from our first book, you're in the right place. No matter your experience, this journey welcomes everyone ready to level up their game.

Welcome to "The Advanced RPG Guide to Becoming an Expert Dungeon Master."

This book is all about leveling up your game mastering, moving from 'Relax, I know what I'm doing' to 'Are you ready to convince flying crabs to join your war against the Ocean of Blood?' Yeah, we're about to crank that dial from competent to wild. You can think of this book as part two, the sequel you didn't know you needed, but trust me, you'll be glad it's here. Keep that previous book close by though (or maybe even grab a copy of it if you're feeling lost) in case you need to remember how to do a funny voice at the absolute worst time.

If, at any point, this book starts to feel like it's throwing too much at you, don't stress. The first guide's still there, waiting like a loyal NPC, ready to step in when things get a bit too chaotic. Sometimes, we all need a moment to get back to basics, especially when those flying crabs start asking complicated moral questions. So take a breath, flip back if you need to, and then jump back into the deep end when you're ready.

Within the pages of this book, I'll be teaching under the assumption that you've already got the basics down. I'm not going to explain what Session Zero is again or walk you through the logistics of wrangling a player who won't stop making inappropriate comments or won't take a shower. We're moving past that. This book is here to take you from running pre-made one-shots to creating vibrant, living worlds and making split-second calls that bring those worlds to life. We're going from level one kobolds to an endgame of dragons, deep conspiracies, and maybe even rewriting the very fabric of your game's universe.

This isn't just about surviving the journey from level one to twenty; it's about thriving in it. It's about creating those unforgettable, late-night sessions where the table goes silent, leaning in, hanging on your every word. It's about turning the dice rolls - those natural 20s and crushing 1s - into stories that echo long after the campaign ends. It's about weaving a tapestry so rich that your players will be retelling the saga for years, maybe even as part of their own stories someday.

So, if you're ready to go beyond the ordinary—to craft unforgettable adventures, breathe life into entire worlds, and turn chaos into narrative gold—then let's dive in. Welcome, fellow Dungeon Master, to the next level. Let's make some magic.

Chapter 1: A Worldbuilding & Homebrewing Crash Course

Worldbuilding is the bedrock of any epic TTRPG - it's the canvas where all the magic, mayhem, and questionable player decisions unfold. And homebrewing? That's the extra shot of espresso that takes it from "good enough" to "awwweee yeah!" The way you wield them is what separates the Dungeon Master Supreme from the Dungeon Master Just-Here-to-Roll-the-Dice.

Trying to cram both worldbuilding and homebrewing into a single chapter is like trying to fit Smaug into a hobbit hole - not happening without a lot of chaos and a ton of stuff getting broken. Which is why we're writing this chapter as a crash course. We've got other books that plunge deep into the nitty-gritty for when you're ready to go full mad-scientist-DM and cackle over your meticulously crafted lore. But for now, let's get your world spinning, your homebrew bubbling, and your players careening through the kind of unpredictable, beautiful madness that leaves scorch marks on the narrative walls.

First up, we're diving into worldbuilding—the good stuff. I'm going to show you why worldbuilding is more than just setting the scene; it's the secret sauce that gets your players so immersed they forget they're sitting at a table and not actually dodging arrows in a haunted forest. You'll get a handful of tips and tricks to kick off your worldbuilding journey, plus some advice on how to keep that world growing as your campaign progresses - because nothing says "realism" like seeing your world change based on what your players do... or what they completely mess up.

Then, we're onto homebrewing. This section is all about taking what's there and twisting it into something unique. I'm going to show you not only how to create some cool homebrew content, but also how it can supercharge your DMing skills because, let's be honest, you're not just here to follow the rules - you're here to bend them, break them, and craft something that makes your players sit up and go, "Wait, we can do that?" You take the premade rules and you turn them all around. That's what it's all about.

Worldbuilding 101

So, what is worldbuilding anyway, and why should you care? In its simplest terms, worldbuilding is exactly what it sounds like: the process of creating an entire fictional world where your campaign, your story, your magic, and all the shenanigans unfold.

It's the space your adventurers get to roam, whether they're exploring ancient ruins, negotiating peace between warring factions, or - yep - convincing those aforementioned flying crabs to join them against the Ocean of Blood. Think of it like setting the stage for a grand play, where every mountain, street, and peculiar local custom helps shape the players' experience.

But why worldbuild at all? Isn't using a pre-made world good enough? The short answer is absolutely. The long answer: well, it depends on what kind of experience you want to create. Established worlds like Faerun or Middle-earth are brilliant, and there's a reason they've become so iconic. They come packed with rich lore, established cities, and powerful NPCs - all ripe for the picking.

But here's the catch: everyone else knows those worlds too. Players might be familiar with the history of Neverwinter or know exactly what's lurking in the Mines of Moria. And while there's certainly a lot of comfort in that familiarity, it can also mean your carefully crafted surprises might fall a bit flat, like trying to make a big reveal when everyone at the table already knows what's behind the curtain.

And that's where worldbuilding becomes the real MVP. By creating your own unique world, you're giving your players something that feels fresh, alive, and unpredictable. You're shaping a place where they have no preconceived notions and where anything can happen.

Imagine the thrill on your players' faces when they realize they're dealing with Foreversummer, not Neverwinter - sure, they might mock you relentlessly for your off-the-cuff renaming (I'm absolutely *not* speaking from experience), but suddenly, they're intrigued. It's new, it's different, and it's entirely yours. Worldbuilding gives you the power to keep players guessing and to surprise them at every twist and turn.

So, how do you start? I'd say the best way to jump into worldbuilding is by starting small - bite-sized pieces are less overwhelming and help keep your creative juices flowing. Choose one aspect that excites you the most: maybe it's the geography (what if your world has an ocean made entirely of fire?) or the culture (what if the king is only a figurehead, and real power rests with a council of talking monkeys?). Start there and see where it takes you.

If you're fascinated by political intrigue, then you should flesh out the major pieces on the political board. If you're a geography geek, get that map started. Don't be afraid to borrow ideas either - worldbuilding is often a remix of concepts that already exist, so find inspiration in the things you love and let them evolve into something new.

Once you have your starting point, expand from there. Let's say you begin with a desert city surrounded by endless dunes. You could start by naming the city and imagining what it looks like. Maybe it's a sprawling mass of dome shaped rooftops with narrow, twisting streets, a labyrinth of market stalls, and a towering palace of sandstone rising above it all - or maybe you built your own desert version of Venice with canals filled with Sahara sand.

Now ask yourself: how does this city survive in the middle of a desert? Where do they get their water? Do they have a magical process of turning sand into water figured out? What's the culture like? Will they latch on to the first guy they see and make him their messiah? Maybe they enjoy thrill-riding the gigantic sandworms who roam their lands?

The key here is to let each idea spark another. Once you've got the city and the wells, you can start thinking about the order of monks who prophesied the messiah's arrival. Who are they? Why are they guarding the water? Are they revered by the city's people or feared? Do they have powers tied to the water source - maybe they can purify it, or maybe they're cursed to never leave the underground tunnels. Each answer you come up with adds depth to your world and gives you more hooks for your players to grab onto.

And here's a little secret: you don't have to have everything figured out right away. Worldbuilding can grow and evolve alongside your campaign. The more questions your players ask, the more you'll be inspired to fill in the blanks. It's a dynamic process, one where you start by knowing just enough to answer the players' immediate questions - and trust me, those questions will come.

"How long has the king ruled?" might just be the simplest question that has ever stumped me into an existential crisis.

One of the best parts about worldbuilding is that it adds depth and richness to the game that pre-made settings sometimes struggle to match. A custom world feels personal, not just to you but to your players. They feel like they're discovering something no one else has ever seen before, which is incredibly rewarding. They become invested in the world because it's a reflection of their actions.

If your players plan to rob the village blind but accidentally end up dropping the loot, and villagers pick it up, will they build a statue of your players and sing folk songs of their heroics? These changes give your players a sense of real impact, something that's harder to achieve when everyone already knows how the story goes.

That's only a snippet of how geography can affect culture, almost every aspect of worldbuilding is connected to each other. A political affiliation can influence the magic system, just like the natural resources may impact the population density.

Of course, it's also important to think about how your world connects to your story. The world should serve as a backdrop that enhances the story, but does not overshadow it. If your players are meant to be heroes, give them a world that needs saving - a place teetering on the edge, with tensions brewing and dangers lurking.

Worldbuilding is not something you have to do on your own, nor is it something you have to do all at once. It is, however, a huge undertaking, so involve your players in the process. Maybe one of them wants their character to come from a distant island kingdom. Instead of building it yourself, ask them what the weather is like there, if they crabfish, or if they build sandcastles daily. Work together to create a piece of the world that they'll feel personally connected to.

When players help shape the world, they're more invested in it, and they're more excited to explore it. It also works in your favor because not only are your players less likely to go off track, but them following your path lessens your workload so you can focus on other aspects of DMing.

Honestly, it solves a whole lot of DM problems, and who doesn't want that?

In the end, worldbuilding is all about creating a setting that enhances the story and gives your players a world they want to dive into and explore. Whether it's a haunted forest, a desolate wasteland, or a sprawling city-state, your world is the stage. It's the ultimate playground for your adventurers to discover who they are and what they're capable of. Just remember - it's not just about creating the world; it's about inviting your players to live in it. How you frame each scene, the details you choose to highlight, and the overall atmosphere you conjure are ultimately what transform a collection of ideas into a world that feels tangible. Make your world a place your players don't just see, but also experience.

Creating a Sense of Space

Creating a sense of space is about more than just telling your players where they are - it's about making your players feel like they're there. A good Dungeon Master doesn't just say, "You're in a forest," and leave it at that. They describe the forest in vivid detail, describing the darkness behind the trees, sounds of howling in the distance, and the scent of the mud caked to their boots to evoke as many of the senses as possible.

17 | A Worldbuilding & Homebrewing Crash Course

Think about it: if you say, "You're in a dark forest," it's easy for players to imagine something generic. But if you say, "You're in a forest where the gnarled trees twist like skeletal fingers, their bark flaking off in long, dry sheets. The air is damp, smelling of moss and decay, and there's a soft rustle just beyond your vision, like something moving through the underbrush," now your players are feeling the tension. They're leaning in. They can almost smell that musty earth, and they can hear whatever is lurking nearby. That's where immersion lives, and that's how you set the tone for what comes next.

Don't just describe what the environment sounds like. Use all five senses to create vivid imagery. Mention the far-off hooting of an owl, the crackling of branches, and the flutter of leaves reaching the ground. And what about the smell? Maybe the air is thick with the scent of pine needles and damp soil, or perhaps there's a hint of smoke on the breeze-an indication that there might be people nearby. What can the players feel? Is the air cold and bitter, or is the ground beneath them uneven and rocky? Even taste can come into play - perhaps they feel the metallic tang of fear in their mouths, or the salty spray from a nearby sea, or maybe a bird was flying overhead, and they decided it would make a nice barbecue.

This kind of imagery doesn't just make the world feel alive - its also a storytelling tool. Let's say your players are in a busy market, and you describe the sound of merchants calling, the laughter of children running by, the clinking of coins, and the rich smells of street food, spices, and freshly baked bread. But then suddenly, amidst all this sensory deluge, they hear one thing that is out of place: a hushed voice whispering their name from the darkness. That jarring sensory contrast creates tension, making the moment stand out in their minds. Using sensory details also gives players clues about the environment and what they might want to do.

If you describe the scent of smoke in the wind, the players may elect to investigate and find a campfire or travelers. If they hear the faint sound of running water, they may decide to head in that direction, hoping to find a stream to refill their canteens. When used this way, sensory clues give players suggestions without smacking them in the head with the obvious. Crafting that vivid sense of place isn't just about the physical descriptors themselves - you have to make them *feel* it and make it pay off in the end.

Do they get a feeling of unease or is it comfortable? Do they feel sheltered and safe or are they exposed? For example, a large open plain has one great vulnerability, both for your party and approaching enemies. There is nowhere to hide; any potential threat can be seen approaching from miles off. In contrast, a narrow alleyway in a sprawling city would be easier to hide in, with the tall buildings blocking out the sky and the cobblestones slick with morning mist. The mood you set with your descriptions can affect how players decide to act as you invite them to engage with the surroundings.

Once you've set the scene, ask them what they want to do. Perhaps they'd like to reach out and touch the bark of that tree you just described or see if they can recognize the strange, sweet smell cutting through the air. The more your players interact, the more real the space is to them, and the deeper into the story they become immersed. If you do things right, you might suffer from success and witness your players wreaking havoc on your world. As the DM who created that world, it's your job to keep track of its chaos and inevitable destruction.

Campaign-Influenced World Evolution

A vibrant, living world isn't static - it shifts and evolves as the campaign unfolds, reflecting the actions (or inactions) of your players. The choices they make should ripple outward, causing a change that's both visible and significant. This is what makes the world feel real, like the actions in it truly matter. But evolution isn't only about what the players do - sometimes, it's also about what they don't do or even the butterfly effect on events happening far away they aren't even aware of.

Imagine your players defeat a local bandit gang that's been terrorizing the nearby villages. Great! But what happens next? Maybe that power vacuum they've created leads to a new rival group stepping up with more resources and ambition to fill the void. Perhaps the villagers, now free, start expanding their settlement, which leads to new trade opportunities - or new conflicts with neighbors who don't appreciate the competition.

These changes show that the world is responding to the players' actions in dynamic ways, giving them a sense of consequence and impact. Their victories, no matter how small, have a lasting influence that shapes the world around them.

And it's not all about success either. Suppose your players hear whispers of a brewing rebellion in the capital city and decide to ignore it, focusing instead on their immediate quest for treasure. A few sessions later, they hear news of the rebellion erupting into full-blown chaos, with the streets of the capital running red, and refugees fleeing to nearby towns - towns that the players frequent, towns that were once bustling but are now overrun and strained under the influx. The very fabric of everyday life shifts, and the players realize that their decision to ignore the unrest had a significant consequence, one that ripples beyond what they could see or control. Changes like those increase immersion because they make the world feel alive and independent of players and their actions.

But it's not just about the players' decisions. The world also evolves in response to other, unrelated events - distant conflicts, natural disasters, shifts in political alliances. Imagine that a neighboring kingdom falls into turmoil. The players are nowhere near the action, but the effects of that war make their way to the players' doorstep. Refugees flee across borders, bringing stories of horror and pleading for help. Trade routes become unstable, with merchant caravans opting for safer roads, leading to increased prices for goods. A noble family in hiding approaches the players, offering them a dangerous job in exchange for a priceless heirloom.

These kinds of events add texture to the world and show that it doesn't revolve entirely around the players - things happen whether they're there or not, and sometimes they're caught in the aftermath. Using these sorts of events is also super convenient when you need to reestablish control over your session, or your players. (You can even call on these distant influences if you forgot what you had planned for the session - which happens to the best of us.) And now, all of a sudden, there's a thunder of dragons raining down upon the world. And yes, 'thunder of dragons' is the proper name for a group of dragons; I did not make it up just because it sounds cool - it's like a murder of crows.

Another powerful way to show world evolution is through the NPCs. When players form bonds with NPCs, those relationships can be a gauge of the world's ongoing changes. Maybe the kindly innkeeper who once offered discounted rooms starts charging more because the influx of refugees has strained his supplies, or maybe a guard captain who was once friendly and lighthearted becomes more hardened and wary after a recent skirmish. The actions of the players can directly shape these relationships, and the changing circumstances of the NPCs serve as reminders of the players' impact.

Evolution can also happen on a small scale. Perhaps the players fail to stop a thief in a bustling city market, and weeks later, they return to find that the marketplace is riddled with a stronger presence of guards, each vendor casting wary glances, and the once-open air is now cloaked in a palpable sense of distrust. Their failure has shifted the atmosphere.

Maybe, alternatively, the thief has grown bolder and now rules the market from the shadows, having used the players' absence to gain power. These micro-evolutions help maintain continuity and make every action - or failure - feel meaningful.

The idea is to let the players see the results of their choices (or lack thereof). It's not just about success or failure; it's about showing that they have left a mark, for better or for worse.

Maybe they cleared a cursed forest, and now the once-spooky trees are giving way to saplings and new life - villagers cautiously exploring new farmland where they once feared to tread. Or perhaps they abandoned a quest, and that forest grew darker still, attracting dangerous beings to fill the void they left behind. The players should feel the consequences, big or small, unfolding around them because the weight of those consequences will add emotional investment and enrich the narrative.

As a Dungeon Master, think about how the outcomes of encounters - whether they're battles, negotiations, or pivotal choices - affect the broader world. What shifts in the power structure? How do NPCs react? How does the environment change?

By reflecting the players' actions in the world around them, you create a campaign that feels rich, interconnected, and deeply immersive. Your players aren't just moving through a static map - they are shaping it, with every quest completed, every enemy spared or slain, every piece of information heeded or ignored.

But what happens when your players' eyes glaze over, and their excitement starts to fizzle out like a flat soda? It's not the world that's stale — it's the *gameplay* that's gone as bland as unsalted porridge. Sounds like it's time to toss in some narrative hot sauce and crank up the flavor.

Homebrewing Your Own Fun

The best way to look at homebrewing is as the secret formula that takes your game from a microwaveable burger to a delicious Krabby Patty. This is where you stop being just a Dungeon Master and become the omniscient, omnipresent, and omnipotent master of the universe. The maker of rules. Whether it's crafting custom spells or even magic systems, building factions based on worshiping a giant blob of goo, or inventing rules that will have your players question their sanity, homebrewing is where your creativity shines in spectacular fashion.

But don't worry, this isn't a trial by fire. I'm here to be your overly enthusiastic guide, the one who hands you the keys to Pandora's box and says, "Go nuts, but, you know, responsibly." In this section, we'll break down the art of homebrewing into manageable pieces, ensuring that what you create is fun, functional, and just unhinged enough to keep your players guessing.

Homebrewing isn't just about flexing your creative muscles either - it's about tailoring the game to your table. Want a low-magic steampunk dystopia where goblins unionize? Done. Need a high-stakes political drama where Santa's elves are the mob bosses? Let's make it happen. The goal is to build a world that fits your players like a perfectly tailored, slightly chaotic suit.

So, grab your dice and your imagination (and maybe some aspirin). We're about to dive headfirst into the beautiful madness of making TTRPGs truly your own. Who knows, maybe we'll find Atlantis, Titanic, or a mute, yet still cute, siren

Crafting Fun & Engaging NPCs

NPCs are the unsung heroes of your campaign - or, depending on your players, the over-sung ones. They're the quirky innkeepers, the mysterious shopkeepers, and the overly dramatic rival adventurers who somehow steal every scene they're in. Done right, NPCs turn your world from a static stage set into a living, breathing ecosystem. Done wrong, they're just quest dispensers with all the charisma of Roz from *Monsters Inc*. Let's make sure yours are the former.

Why bother homebrewing NPCs, you ask? Well, because you're not just a Dungeon Master - you're a worldbuilder, a storyteller, and occasionally the cruel puppet master pulling the strings of doom. NPCs are your chance to inject life into your world, to give your players someone to laugh with, cry over, or despise with the fiery passion usually reserved for the "buffering" wheel during the reunion episode of *Real Housewives of Beverly Hills,* while the router flickers with a smug little green light, pretending everything's fine.

They're the mortar holding the bricks of your game together. Without them, your players are just a group of murder hobos looting increasingly empty dungeons.

But here's the twist: creating an NPC isn't some arcane ritual. It's more like making a sandwich... that occasionally threatens your party and becomes the surprise big bad. Whether you're prepping a major NPC weeks in advance or inventing one on the fly because your rogue decided to pickpocket the baker (*again*), the process is the same. Give them a hook, tie them to the world, and make them just weird enough to be memorable.

Let's say you've got an upcoming session in which the party is heading to a bustling port city. You decide to prep a fishmonger NPC because every bustling port city needs one, right? Now, you could just name him Bob and call it a day, but where's the fun in that? Instead, give him a hook. Maybe he's a retired pirate who misses the high seas and insists on naming every fish after his old crewmates. "Ah, this here's Captain Haddock—real mean cod, that one. And don't get me started on First Mate Salmon!" Boom. Instant character.

But what if your players decide to bypass your lovingly crafted fishmonger and instead interrogate the random street vendor selling knockoff potions? This is where improvisation shines. Using the same logic, you whip up a quick hook. The potion vendor has an overly cheerful demeanor but keeps nervously glancing over their shoulder.

Why? Because they're on the run from the city's alchemist guild after botching a love potion that caused an accidental city-wide pigeon riot. It's ridiculous, but now your players are hooked - and so is the vendor, who's probably about to join the party.

It should be worth remembering that NPCs need imperfections, the little details that make them feel real and relatable. Think of your favorite fictional characters. Are they flawless goody-two-shoes? No. They're lovable messes. Frodo wouldn't be half as interesting without his crippling self-doubt, and Jack Sparrow's entire brand is being a charismatic train wreck.

Your NPCs don't need to be perfect; they just need to feel alive. Maybe the fishmonger has an irrational fear of crabs and yells, "The pincers!" every time one gets too close. Maybe the potion vendor is allergic to half the ingredients in their own stock. It's quirks like this that make them stick in your players' minds.

Of course, there's always the debate: should you plan your NPCs in advance or just wing it? Prepared NPCs are like that perfect playlist you curate for a road trip - everything's in place, and it feels seamless. You can give them rich backstories, complex motivations, and intricate ties to your world.

But what happens when your players decide to take a metaphorical U-turn and head into the random forest you didn't plan for? That's where improv NPCs shine. They're your game's Spotify DJ mode. Sometimes, you hit a banger, sometimes, it's... less than that... but most of the time they can just act as the background noise on a long car ride.

Here's the kicker, though: it doesn't matter whether an NPC was planned in advance or created on the fly. Players won't care if you spent three hours crafting the perfect enigmatic wizard or three seconds naming the local blacksmith "Thud." What they care about is whether the NPC feels real, whether they spark curiosity, and whether they make the world feel alive.

The best part is that NPCs are like jigsaw puzzle pieces - you can always swap them in and out as needed. That shady potion vendor who barely existed five minutes ago? If the players love them, you can flesh them out later, maybe tying them to a larger guild of rogue alchemists. If they don't? Toss them into the pile of NPCs nobody remembers, right next to "generic barmaid" and "third goblin from the left."

The trick is to treat every NPC, no matter how minor, as a potential masterpiece. Not all of them will land, and that's fine. Some will get a passing glance, while others will become campaign-defining figures - looking at you, Fred the Vampire Accountant. But whether they're a five-minute invention or a five-hour masterpiece, the process is the same: give them a hook, a connection, and a dash of imperfection. And if all else fails, remember this: any NPC can become unforgettable if they yell "My cabbages!" at the right moment.

Creating Loot

Loot is the ultimate motivator - it is the glistening treasure that keeps adventurers diving headfirst into dark caves, facing down monsters twice their size, and getting into more trouble than Bilbo Baggins at a jewelry convention. From glittering gold coins to lightsabers, loot isn't just a pile of goodies; it's the fuel that makes the TTRPG machine purr. Or, you know, sputter and scream, depending on how generous you're feeling.

But the most important thing you need to remember about loot is that it's more than just giving your players stuff - it is about creating incredible moments. Think of Indiana Jones solving the weight pressure plate puzzle and then promptly running from the giant rolling ball. That is *exactly* what you want.

So, why make custom loot when official sources already offer tons of it? Because custom loot is your way of putting a personal stamp on your game. It's like giving your players an Easter egg hunt but with flamethrowers and magic helmets.

Anyone can toss in a generic +1 sword, but what about The Sword of Inexplicable Sass? It's got a bonus to attack rolls and also occasionally heckles its wielder with comments like, "Are you aiming for the goblins or the wall?

Well, you coulda fooled me!" Suddenly, loot is not just loot - it's a character, it's humorous, and it's a moment that your players will remember long after the campaign is over.

Take a page from your favorite pop culture loot: The Elder Wand wasn't just a flashy stick - it was a curse, a death magnet, and a wand that came with more baggage than a baggage claim. Custom loot tells a story. It says, "Hey, adventurer, you didn't just find a shiny rock - you found a shiny rock somehow integral to defeating a dragon. Or it just might make you reveal your deepest, darkest, most embarrassing secrets when romancing an NPC." It's your chance to hand your players an item that's more than a stat boost - it's a part of the narrative.

Imagine your players stumble upon a mysterious chest. They fling it open, expecting the usual pile of gold and sparkly loot, but instead, they find Thor's Drinking Horn. This bad boy lets them drink endlessly without ever suffering a hangover - pure bliss. But there's a catch: it also fills them with an unshakeable sense of self-importance. Sure, they get a bonus to Charisma checks, but only if they puff out their chests like they're auditioning for a godly beer commercial and occasionally give their belly a self-satisfied pat.

The loot itself becomes an extension of your players' personalities. Your dwarf barbarian now feels like Thor on a bender, and the cleric is already preparing Greater

Restoration for the inevitable next morning when the player realizes he challenged an orc to an arm-wrestling match.

Creating custom loot isn't just about the power it gives players - it's also about the flavor. When Captain America picked up Mjolnir, the entire cinema audience lost their collective minds, and that is the exact kind of loot reaction we're aiming for. Whether it's a weapon that sings Eye of the Tiger every time a crit hits or a cloak that makes you invisible only when nobody is looking at you, these items turn ordinary loot drops into spectacular moments.

And don't just stop at the big stuff. Sometimes, the smallest loot makes the biggest impact. Just remember the stuff McGyver could do with a paperclip. The little things matter.

The best part of custom loot is the opportunity to blend the familiar with the fantastical. Picture your players finding The Sunglasses of Neo's Nonchalance - they grant incredible insight and dodging skills, but only to players that never show emotion and dramatically remove the shades mid-conversation. Giving players loot that's clearly inspired by something familiar they know and love invites them to laugh, groan, or embrace the drama, just like their favorite characters did while also adding to the world's overall lore.

But it's not all fun and games - sometimes the loot is cursed, and sometimes it's cursed in ways that would make even the most benevolent DM cackle. You want loot that's tempting, like the mirror of deepest desires- powerful, alluring, but ultimately dangerous. What about The Crown of the Mad Titan? It gives its wearer the strength of ten ogres, but slowly replaces their sense of empathy with a deep, Thanos-like certainty that they know what's best for everyone.

Cursed items make your players ask themselves if whatever they're about to do is actually worth it. And that's the kind of storytelling gold we live for. Just picture your paladin, now corrupted by the crown, giving a snap-worthy monologue about balance while the rest of the party looks for a way to "accidentally" knock it off his head.

Loot isn't the only thing you can custom-make to add flavor or a personal touch to a party - you can "forge" your own custom equipment. I personally enjoy giving my players something they can use all the time. Like, for example, a Ring of Fire Resistance is cool, but how often are you *really* going to be on fire? Maybe "Sneak Sabatons" that add +2 to Stealth would be more appreciated.

Custom Equipment

Custom equipment is like Hermione's bag of holding: endlessly useful and organized — while custom loot is like the Marauder's Map, revealing wild possibilities and offering mischief around every corner. Where custom loot is all about that sweet, sparkly reward - the kind of thing that makes your players feel like they've just pulled the Master

Sword from its pedestal - custom equipment is more grounded, more practical. It's the stuff that gets your players through their day-to-day lives in the game.

Custom loot is often the shiny treasure at the end of the rainbow, but custom equipment is the bread and butter - the gear your players wield, wear, and trust. It's the battle-worn armor, the well-balanced sword, the favorite crossbow that never jams.

This is the kind of stuff that makes the players feel like their characters are evolving in more ways than just having a new toy that lights up and goes pew pew. Custom equipment is where you get to really dive in and add that personal touch, like the perfect accessories to a cosplay - accurate, useful, and tailored to fit the character's style but much less expensive and easier to make.

One of my favorite applications of custom loot happened when a player was dissatisfied with a sword he got at the beginning of the game. Since it didn't make much narrative sense to just pluck it out of the game and insert a new one, I made an NPC blacksmith that promised him a really overpowered one but that the sword could only be made from a special type of metal, thus creating the whole sidequest for him. Giving this material to the blacksmith and then walking out with a shiny new sword (and additional equipment for the rest of the team) gave them all the sense of satisfaction they craved.

Where custom loot is about rewards for grand accomplishments, custom equipment is often about practicality and adaptation.

Your players are setting off into an arctic tundra for the first time? Great! Instead of just telling them, "Roll survival checks until you freeze or find some hot cocoa," you can give them the opportunity to prepare themselves.

Maybe they meet a tinkerer who can add retractable spikes to their boots for better traction or a local artisan who makes fur-lined cloaks to keep out the cold. Maybe they come across an innkeeper with a special brew to "keep them warm on the inside." By giving them options like this, you're adding realism to the world and letting your players feel prepared and capable, turning what could be a routine trek into a more immersive experience.

These pieces of custom equipment make the players feel prepared, and they give the world more texture. Suddenly, it's not just "the cold north"; it's a place with culture, ingenuity, and flavor. Now your players aren't just checking off survival rolls - they're leaning into the narrative of how they're conquering the elements with the help of some quirky locals and a bit of ingenuity.

Of course, custom equipment also means embracing the wild requests that your players throw at you like you're their personal Q from James Bond. (And let's be honest, isn't that half the fun?)

Maybe the barbarian wants a shield that doubles as a sled so they can escape down the hillside from an angry frost giant. Or the bard wants a lute that doubles as a war axe, because nothing says "multitasking" like playing a metal solo and chopping down an enemy in one smooth motion. Or maybe the rogue just binged Assassin's Creed and wants retractable daggers that slide out of their sleeves. And yes, before you ask, I really had to create all of these for my players, they are annoying and demanding but I love them dearly.

My point? Saying yes to these requests (within reason) can do wonders for your game. It keeps the players engaged, encourages them to think creatively, and makes the world feel alive and responsive. When your players come to you with an idea, and you not only roll with it but find ways to make it interesting, they'll be even more invested in how they use their gear.

Plus, it's a golden opportunity for comedic moments. I mean, nothing says *D&D* like a rogue trying to impress everyone with their new hidden dagger, only to misfire and skewer a nearby bar stool.

That said, balance is key. The goal is to make custom equipment useful, memorable, and fun - not to make your players feel like they've all got Tony Stark's Hulkbuster armor at level three. Sure, the wizard might want an enchanted robe that grants fire resistance, but if that robe ends up making them feel invincible against every flaming threat, you've essentially given them a get-out-of-dragons-free card.

The trick is to craft items that fit the narrative and provide practical benefits without making every encounter a cakewalk. A fireproof robe is great, but maybe you have to roll a d4 every time before you use to see how many minutes the effects will last. Ultimately, custom equipment is all about customization and about giving your players something that's theirs, something that helps tell their story. Whether it's the arctic cloak that reminds them of their harrowing journey across the tundra or a bard's war axe-lute combo that's just as likely to chop as it is to charm, these items make the ordinary feel extraordinary.

Custom equipment is great for giving players the right tools for the job, but custom spells are where you really get to bend the rules of reality. When players want to do more than just hit harder (they want to turn enemies green, float themselves above the battlefield defying gravity, or maybe even just become popular...lar) custom spells are how you let them break the world in ways that are creative, unpredictable, and unmistakably their own.

Custom Magic Systems

Homebrewing a magic system is a lot like building a whole world - it's got to have rules, structure, and enough character to make even Gandalf raise an eyebrow. Just like your world needs geography, cultures, and politics, your magic system needs its own laws, sources, and boundaries.

If you're already crafting an entire world, it only makes sense to think about how magic fits in - where it comes from, how it works, and, most importantly, how it messes with all the other bits you've painstakingly built. Think of it like setting up Wi-Fi - everyone relies on it, everyone complains when it drops, but only a handful of omnipotent wizards truly know why it decides to vanish when you decide to ditch movie night with your parter to play videogames (go spend some time with them, I'm sure it will turn back on as soon as they want to use it.)

A magic system is, at its core, the set of rules that govern how magic works in your world. Is magic a rare, mystical force that only a select few can wield, or is it as common as Instagram influencers selling makeup products and pumping out outrageous brand deals? Does magic derive from dusty old tomes, divine blessings, elemental forces, or just sheer stubborn willpower?

These are the questions you need to answer when you're building your magic system. Consistency is key here - your players need to understand the "how" and "why" of magic. No one likes a system that feels like it's being made up on the fly. The aim is to give magic a framework that feels natural, so your players know what's possible and, more importantly, what might just blow up in their faces.

Speaking of balance, creating a well-balanced magic system is even more critical than the balance of frosting on cake. Too much, and it's overwhelming; too little, and it's not fun anymore. You want your magic system to add depth and flavor to the world without turning one character into Dumbledore and the rest into first year Neville Longbottoms. A balanced magic system keeps things exciting and challenging for everyone. There's nothing worse than having one player annihilate every challenge with a flick of their wrist while everyone else just awkwardly watches.

Think of magic as less of a winning lottery ticket and more of a credit card with a dangerously high limit. Sure, you can hurl fireballs now, but sooner or later, the bill - and the consequences - are going to come knocking.

Magic should come with a price - whether it's physical exhaustion, a shred of your soul, or the awkward social fallout of casting spells that are rightfully frowned upon. Magic should feel earned, not handed out like cheap Costco hotdogs. Watching your players sweat over the consequences of summoning a demon while the local guards are already twitchy about unsanctioned magic? That's the kind of drama we live for.

Think of magic as a finite resource with real-world consequences. Sure, that fireball just turned a roomful of enemies into crispy critters, but now the floor's charred, the air's a swirling vortex of smoke, and the druid's hacking like they just swallowed a bonfire. When the rogue's still waving away smoke ten minutes later and the bard's muttering about their cloak's tragic demise, you know you've made magic more than just a flashy damage roll.

Magic should leave an imprint on the world, one that lingers and inconveniences everyone, not just the caster. It's not just about who took the most damage - it's about the collateral chaos. The kind where someone's eyebrows are permanently singed and someone else is wondering why they smell like burnt toast.

And look, I get it. Maybe all this magic talk is making the non-spellcasters in the room feel left out. Not every campaign needs wizards zapping lightning bolts every five minutes to be fun. But when magic is in the mix, make sure it's as wondrous, chaotic, and gloriously messy as it deserves to be.

One of the best things about homebrewing a magic system is that you don't have to start from scratch. Why reinvent the wand when you can borrow one from another game? If you find a magic system in another TTRPG that fits your vibe, steal it - tweak it, twist it, and reforge it in the fires of your own campaign world. Maybe you love the wild, chaotic flavor of Mage: The Ascension or the gritty, tech-infused sorcery of Shadowrun.

Who says those systems have to stay locked within their original games? Magic is magic, and in the realm of homebrew, all spells are fair game. Adapt the rules you like, strip away what doesn't work, and give your players a magical experience that feels fresh but familiar.

Once, I was hyped to run a Shadowrun game - cyberpunk cities, neon-drenched alleys, and magic flickering alongside malfunctioning tech. The problem? I didn't have the Shadowrun rules on hand, and my players were already on their way, expecting some chrome-fueled chaos.

So, I grabbed my trusty D&D spell system, gave it a cybernetic facelift, and threw everyone into a gritty future where wizards hacked reality with glitchy mana programs and street shamans summoned spirits through AR overlays. Instead of fireballs, they hurled digital pyrotechnics that fried enemy circuits. Instead of spell slots, they ran on 'mana batteries' that could short out if overused. It wasn't perfect, but it was glorious. We had firewalls burning, drones exploding, and the rogue nearly got arrested for trying to 'counterspell' a traffic light. Moral of the story? It's okay (and often far easier) to have a starting point. The system is still yours even if you "borrowed" it to retweak to fit your needs. Sometimes, you don't need the perfect system - you just need a system that works right now.

Custom Technology

Sometimes, you don't want to slay dragons and wield magic. I get that. Sometimes it's about battling megacorps with cyber enhanced chaos. That's right, we're about to venture into the wonderfully maddening world of homebrewing custom technology for your sci-fi settings.

If you've already tackled custom loot, equipment, and magic systems, you probably think you've got this down, right? Well, sort of. See, while the concept of adding custom elements to your game might seem straightforward, when you swap out "magic" for "technology," things start to get a bit... weird. Unlike magic, which can be its own mysterious force with zero regard for Newton's laws, technology tends to come with some strings attached - namely, the laws of physics and the ever-watchful eyes of those players who just know too much about how quantum mechanics should work.

So, let's address the big difference right out of the gate: magic is essentially a free-for-all. You want a fireball that can set a dragon's pajamas ablaze while simultaneously turning everyone's hair pink? Cool, it's magic - it can do whatever you want it to. You're only limited by your imagination.

Technology, however, doesn't get that kind of freedom, at least not in a sci-fi setting. If you create an anti-gravity toaster, your players will want to know how it works. And you're gonna have an answer to that question - or at least make it look like you considered it. A well-designed piece of custom tech needs to feel like it could, in some way, exist within the universe you're building. Or at least be *somewhat* scientifically plausible, just enough to keep players immersed.

Now, does that mean you have to be some sort of scientist who understands particle accelerators and quantum entanglement just to put a shiny new gizmo in your players' hands? Absolutely not. But it does mean that your anti-gravity toaster shouldn't be just "because it's cool." There's got to be a reason it works - or at least some technobabble that can keep your players off your back. If they are laymen (let's face it, a whole lot of us sci-fi enthusiasts are), you can use some scientific-sounding phrases like, "It manipulates the localized Higgs field to reduce gravitational influence," with an air of confidence that suggests you definitely didn't just pull that from thin air. Trust me, nine times out of ten, the players will nod, go "oh," and roll with it. And the tenth time? Well, that's what DM discretion is for. Some mysteries are better left unsolved.

One of the best approaches to homebrewing custom technology is thinking about what problem the tech is trying to solve or what narrative purpose it serves. Let's say you need a way for your party to traverse a hostile alien desert -

like, a desert so brutal even the sand itself seems mad at you. Sure, you could invent a force field that keeps out the toxic sandstorms, but consider the realism angle. Instead of the typical "It's a magic shield, but, like, techie," maybe it's an electromagnetic barrier that repels the ionized particles in the sand. Sounds kind of believable, right? Plus, it gives the players something more to think about: "Oh, no, the power cells are getting low! Should we push on or risk getting sandblasted into oblivion?"

I know it's *super hard* to believe, but not all sci-fi has to lean into hard science. There's always the lovely, almost whimsical sub-genre called science fantasy. Star Wars is the quintessential example of it. When you think about the technology in that galaxy far, far away - lightsabers, hyperdrives, droids with personalities - we tend not to care about the real-world science behind it but instead the in-world explanation. We don't question how lightsabers work beyond "kyber crystals and space magic" because Star Wars operates in a place that's half grounded in reality and half totally fantastical. If you're playing a science fantasy game, embrace that looseness. If someone asks why your space elevator runs on "subatomic resonance energy," the only real answer you need is, "Because it's cool, and it moves the story forward."

But let's say you're committed to hard sci-fi - the kind where every player is a mini Neil deGrasse Tyson, waiting to call you out on your lack of astrophysical know-how. In that case, you want your tech to have rules, limitations, and consequences. If the party's starship has a faster-than-light drive, there's got to be something balancing it out - maybe it's risky, or maybe it requires exotic fuel that they'll need to negotiate with a shady alien smuggler to obtain.

Every piece of technology should add to the world and make it feel more alive because the tech isn't just there to look shiny and do cool things - it affects how people live, work, fight, and die. It can open up new gameplay options, but it can also introduce new complications. Players want to use their shiny new plasma rifle? Cool, but remember, it overheats after a few shots, and replacement parts are rare outside of major spaceports.

And don't forget - sometimes the best tech has unintended consequences. That anti-gravity toaster might be perfect for making breakfast in space, but who knew the anti-gravity field also interferes with the ship's navigation systems? Suddenly, what seemed like a straightforward piece of gear is now a plot point. The more you intertwine technology with the world, the more it becomes part of the story, not just a tool.

So, when you're homebrewing custom technology, the key is to find that balance. You want your tech to feel cool, you want it to serve your narrative, and, above all, you want it to feel like it belongs in your setting.

Whether you're going full hard sci-fi or just vibing in that sweet science fantasy space, the technology you create should have just enough depth to keep the players interested without bogging them down in detail. After all, the best parts of the game come not from the tech itself but from how the players interact with it - solving problems, getting into trouble, and, yes, even finding out what happens when you try to use a malfunctioning anti-gravity toaster in zero-G.

Custom Spells

Magic is great and all, but sometimes the spells in the rulebook feel as bland as a slice of untoasted white bread. Maybe your wizard wants to channel some Ghostbusters energy and summon a gooey, sentient slime trap. Perhaps your bard insists on a spell that works like a memory-wiping flash from Men in Black, erasing memories of bad performances or cringe-worthy puns.

That's where homebrewing custom spells comes in. This is your chance to let creativity run wild, bend the rules of reality, and give your players - or villains - spells as unique as they are ridiculous. The trick is balancing power, flavor, and the occasional unintended chaos.

Let's be honest here: official spells are reliable, and while they get you from point A to point B, they don't have that custom magic touch. Maybe they don't fit the vibe of your setting, and maybe they're missing that wild twist your players came up with, or maybe - just maybe - you want a spell that rains chickens down on your players when they make a dumb decision. Why? Who cares why, you are in charge, this is your world, you do what you want, when you want, who you want!

This is where homebrewed spells come to the rescue. It's your playground, your chance to expand magic to fit the plot, the world, or just whatever crazy nonsense your players have conjured in their chaotic little minds. You're the DM. If you say there's a fireball big enough to barbeque a dragon or an illusion spell that makes an entire battalion believe their pants have been stolen by ghosts, then so be it. Homebrewed spells are your ticket to making the magic... magical again.

But let's not get carried away here. While custom spells are fantastic for adding flavor to your campaign, you should still strive to maintain balance. Remember, the mechanics of the game are there for a reason.

Sure, role-playing is about storytelling and fun, but those rules keep the fun fair for everyone. After all, what's an adventure without a little challenge? If the wizard can snap their fingers and vaporize the big bad before the climactic fight even starts, where's the drama in that? A balanced campaign is the difference between "epic, nail-biting showdown" and "Monty Python running away gags, but every five minutes."

So when you're thinking of conjuring up a new spell, ask yourself: How does it fit into the world? What's the cost of casting it? Could it be abused in ways that make your players as overpowered as Geralt of Rivia with unlimited potions and zero consequences? Think of it like cooking - you want the new spice to enhance the dish, not turn it into an inedible mess that leaves your players wondering why the goblin chef thought ghost pepper was a good addition to the quiche.

And hey, I know—it's easy to get overly ambitious when making new spells. You want your players to feel powerful, to pull off the big, flashy moves that make them feel like rock stars - but even the coolest spell should come with its limitations. Maybe it needs a rare component - something so bizarre they have to go on a quest just to get it. Maybe it takes a ridiculous amount of time to cast, so the party has to fend off the baddies in an epic holding action. Or maybe there's a hilarious side effect, like the caster accidentally unleashing an uncontrollable symphony of trumpet-like sounds from their dairy-aire. You know, for balance - and comedy, because as funny as those sounds may be, goodluck passing a stealth check anytime soon.

The point is that custom spells should add something to the game that's fun, fits the story, and gives everyone at the table something to laugh, strategize, or gasp about. Let them be epic, let them be unique - but remember that too much power without the checks and balances just turns your hero into a villain... or worse, a bad punchline. So, go ahead and create those spells that make your players feel like gods - just don't forget to make them work for it. And maybe fidget a bit along the way.

Now that we've brewed up some custom spells, let's take the cauldron a step further and cook up an entire magic system—because why stop at one spell when you can rewrite the very fabric of reality? See, I *told* you this was the Expert Guide.

Custom Classes and Races

Creating custom classes and races is like free-climbing the game design mountain, and the handholds are made of dice. Before you start, you need to know one crucial thing: this is going to rely heavily on the core mechanics of your game system.

Knowing the game inside and out is non-negotiable here. You've got to understand how it ticks, how the gears intertwine, and, most importantly, how to keep those gears from exploding into a million pieces when you add your homebrewed ideas into the mix.

When you're homebrewing a custom class, you're basically creating a new set of rules, abilities, and growth potential that exists entirely within the game's mechanical framework. Think of it like the parts of a car. You've got to make sure the engine (the core game mechanics) works with all the new features you add, like the seat heaters and cup holders (extra content). The class abilities, power scaling, role in combat, and synergy with existing abilities all need to be airtight. Your new class needs to fit into the game without breaking it, either by being grossly overpowered or utterly useless.

On the other hand, homebrewing a custom race is less about mechanics and more about the game world. When you create a new race, you're adding a whole culture, a history, maybe even an entire biome or home planet, depending on your setting. This means you get to flex those creative muscles. What do they eat? How do they interact with the rest of the world? What are their common relationships to others?

But let's not get too loose here - mechanics still do matter. Your custom race still needs game stats, right? So, make sure to balance the physical traits, abilities, potential resistances, and maybe even drawbacks to keep things interesting. While, admittedly, races are more about the lore, there's still a healthy dose of mechanical nuance to keep in mind.

Of course, both custom classes and races impact both the game world and its mechanics. Creating a new class might influence the lore - like, why does this shadowy order of poison-wielding monks exist, and how does the rest of society feel about them?

Conversely, adding a new race with a natural resistance to magic could have huge mechanical implications, especially in a magic-heavy campaign. As you brew these things up, you'll soon see it's an intricate dance between narrative cohesion and game logic. So let me be your instructor, and let's get to classes.

Homebrewing Custom Classes

Homebrewing a custom class is all about balance — hitting that sweet spot between boring and game-breaking. The goal is to create something that fills a unique niche without stepping on the toes of existing classes. Maybe your players want a ranged healer or a high-skill warrior. Identify what's missing in your current lineup and build something that enhances the game without overshadowing whats already there.

A good starting point is to find an existing class as a template and tweak it. If you're building a new class that's about manipulating shadows, maybe start with a rogue or warlock stat sheet and modify from there. Look at what makes those classes balanced (their hit dice, their proficiency bonuses, the rate at which they gain new features - all of it) because mimicking this kind of structure will help keep your creation balanced.

Then, you can add your custom flavor: a particular set of skills that feels distinct but still makes sense in the game's ecosystem. Just remember, giving your new class fifteen different abilities by level three is probably overkill, so remember to pace yourself.

Homebrewing a custom class starts with one core question: What's missing from the game that your players crave? Maybe your campaign is drenched in cosmic horror, but none of the existing classes capture that creeping, sanity-draining vibe.

Enter the Voidcaller: a class that bargains with the abyss, wielding powers that threaten to unravel reality (and their own minds). You take the framework of a warlock but crank the dial toward madness. Their spell slots replenish by absorbing fragments of their own sanity, and instead of patrons, they're tethered to unfathomable entities whose influence manifests as eerie mutations - think extra eyes, shadowy appendages, or whispers only they can hear. Their powers are devastating, but every ability pushes them closer to the brink. Want a tentacle burst that shreds enemies in a 15-foot radius? Sure, but roll a Wisdom save afterward to avoid running nude down the street screaming about "cat overloads ruling from the stars".

Balancing a custom class is where the real alchemy happens. For every absurd power you grant, you need an equally compelling drawback. The Voidcaller can tap into forbidden knowledge to cast any spell they've ever seen, but using it burns away fragments of their memory, leaving gaps in their past - "Wait, why did I swear vengeance on the mayor?"

Balance isn't just about numbers; it's about risks that feel meaningful and consequences that bite. Test it with your group in a one-shot first. Let the player go wild, break things, exploit loopholes, and then trim the excess fat. If the class feels powerful but fragile, like it's walking a razor's edge between heroism and self-destruction, congratulations - you've just brewed up a class that's ready to wreak havoc at your table.

But sometimes, the class isn't the only thing that needs a fresh coat of creativity - what if your world demands heroes (or horrors) who don't quite fit the standard molds of elf ears and dwarf beards?

Homebrewing Custom Races

If your players have ever looked at the standard fantasy races and decided being an elf or dwarf just isn't cutting it, then it's time to unleash the wild, the weird, and the questionably plausible by diving headfirst into homebrewing custom races. When creating a new race, ask yourself what makes them unique. Do they have a particular way of seeing the world? Are they amphibious mushroom people with a telepathic hive mind? Either way, the trick is to make sure their narrative uniqueness translates into balanced game mechanics.

You'll need to decide on a few key things - stat bonuses, racial abilities, languages, and maybe even a drawback or two. Don't shy away from giving your race something quirky that's both beneficial and challenging. For example, maybe your amphibious mushroom people can breathe underwater (which is pretty darn awesome), but they also need to stay moist, or they start taking penalties (better pack that spray bottle). This keeps things balanced and gives players a chance to roleplay around their race's unique traits.

The big challenge with custom races is ensuring they don't completely overshadow the existing options. If your new race is a little too perfect - like, say, they've got a bonus to every ability score and immunity to magic - they're going to make other player choices feel bland by comparison. Instead, focus on giving them distinct, flavorful abilities that make them fun to play without necessarily making them better in every situation. Maybe they're resistant to cold damage because they evolved in a frozen wasteland, but that might also mean they have a lower tolerance for heat.

Finally, consider how your new race fits into your world. Where do they come from? How do they interact with other races? Do they have natural allies or rivals? Giving your players an idea of how their new character fits into the bigger picture will help them create backstories and motivations that enrich your campaign.

Let's say your world has been torn apart by cataclysmic storms, and you want a race born from the chaos itself - meet the Stormforged. These beings aren't just touched by the elements; they are the elements, formed from swirling tempests and lightning-charged clouds.

Picture tall, wiry figures with hair that crackles like static and eyes that flash like distant lightning. They don't walk so much as they drift, feet barely touching the ground, leaving faint traces of mist and ozone in their wake.

Mechanically, give them a natural resistance to thunder and lightning damage and a once-per-long-rest ability to unleash a burst of storm energy, jolting nearby enemies with electric fury. Maybe they don't need to breathe air because, honestly, who needs lungs when your body is 70% vapor and 30% sass?

But don't just stop at flashy powers - give them a cultural hook that ties them into your world. Maybe the Stormforged are seen as living omens, both revered and feared. They might be nomads who travel with the storms, setting up temporary sanctuaries where the lightning dances most fiercely. Perhaps they have no written language, just ephemeral symbols drawn in frost and dissipating vapor, messages that vanish like whispers in the wind.

When your players meet a Stormforged NPC, they're not just meeting a creature - they're encountering the raw, unfiltered chaos of nature itself, wrapped in a sentient package. That's the kind of homebrewed race that makes your world feel alive, electrifying, and just a little dangerous.

Homebrewing custom classes and races is both an art and a science. It's about making something new and exciting while respecting the delicate balance of the game. Whether you're crafting a tech-slinging cybernetic ranger or a clan of lightning-worshipping sky dwarves, make sure the mechanics and lore support each other. Just remember: your players are going to find ways to break it no matter what, so just do your best and enjoy the ride. After all, a little chaos is what makes homebrewing worth it.

Making Custom Characters for Your Players

I know what some of you are thinking: "But isn't character creation the players' job?" And sure, if you've got a table full of seasoned adventurers, they'll probably revel in the process of min-maxing and choosing the perfect background for their chaotic neutral catfolk bard. But when you've got brand-new players - or just that one friend who's overwhelmed by the sheer number of options - it's a good idea to have a few pre-made characters ready to go.

The biggest reason why you would want to make characters in advance is because you want to get people playing as soon as possible. Nothing kills momentum like adding another hour to Session Zero explaining ability scores, spell slots, or the pros and cons of being proficient in sleight of hand versus athletics. To new players, a character sheet filled with boxes, numbers, and obscure abbreviations looks about as inviting as a furniture assembly instruction manual written in Klingon. (Yes, I know some of you can read Klingon, you are very cool, don't let anyone tell you otherwise.)

So, having a few characters ready can take that stress off their shoulders and let them dive straight into the fun part - making questionable decisions and rolling dice to justify them.

Now, just because you're making a character in advance doesn't mean it has to be generic. Actually, that's the opposite of what you should be going for. The idea here is to create something that fits like a glove right off the bat, like a lockpick set that fits perfectly in your rogue's palm or a sword that balances just right in your fighter's grip. The goal is to craft a character that's ready to go and fits seamlessly into the chaos your player brings to the table.

The easiest way to go about this is to think of the person making the request - their quirks, interests, or even the way they approach games in general. You're not creating a character in a vacuum; you're building something that slots perfectly into the way they play.

Maybe they're the type to sit back quietly, calculating everything before striking, like a rogue who lurks in the shadows until the perfect moment to stab arrives, or a cleric who bides their time with quiet wisdom before delivering a divine smackdown of justice. Picture them sneaking through a dimly lit dungeon, rolling their eyes while the rest of the party causes chaos. This isn't just a character; it's their character.

On the flip side, maybe your player is the loud, brash, "kick down the door first, ask questions never" type. This is prime barbarian territory, complete with reckless swings and battle cries that are one part enthusiasm and two parts impending headache. Or maybe they're a fighter who insists on doing everything with a dramatic flourish, from unsheathing their sword with a theatrical twirl to declaring, mid-battle, that this is their defining moment. Think of the player who absolutely needs to make an entrance every time, and give them a character who's just as extra as they are.

And don't forget those players who live for role-play, the ones who can spend an entire session getting lost in character backstory. For them, build a character with layers - the bard who's on a quest to out-sing their bitter rival, or the druid who's fiercely protective of a plot of land because they once lost a beloved mushroom there. Give them hooks, conflicts, and a chance to deliver a heartfelt monologue while the rest of the table tries not to cry.

In short, the more you match the character to the player's vibe, the more they'll feel like they're slipping into something tailor-made rather than squeezing into someone else's armor. Because in the end, whether it's a sneaky rogue, a grandstanding fighter, or a bard with a vendetta, the best characters are the ones that make your players feel like they're exactly where they're meant to be.

This is where knowing your players (or taking some educated guesses) really pays off. The more the character fits their personality or playstyle, the faster they'll feel at home in the game. You want the character to be something they can immediately latch onto, even if it's just one memorable trait - like a paladin who's sworn to uphold the very obscure laws of their tiny village, or a wizard who thinks all the schools of magic are just, frankly, a little tacky... except his own of course.

Creating On the Fly

If you didn't have time to make a character in advance, fear not. With a little practice, you can throw together a character on the fly that's still (or at least feels) tailored to the player. Think of it as the tabletop equivalent of tossing together a surprisingly good meal from leftovers in your fridge - a dash of improvisation, a pinch of intuition, and boom, you've got a character who's ready to roll. The secret here is speed, simplicity, and asking a few questions. "Do you want to be sneaky or smashy?" "Are you into spells, swords, or both?" Their answers will quickly steer you toward the right vibes.

From there, grab a blank character sheet and fill in the essentials: race, class, a few key stats, and a quick background hook. Don't stress about getting every number perfect. Most new players won't care if their Wisdom is an 11 instead of a 12 or if their starting gear isn't a min-maxer's dream. What they will care about is whether they can jump into the game quickly and start having fun. After all, they're more interested in bribing the town guard with that mysterious hunk of cheese they picked up off the floor than in fine-tuning their stat modifiers. The goal is to get them playing, not give them perfect stats.

To make this quick-build character feel real, slap on a unique quirk right off the bat. Maybe they're a ranger who gets into heated arguments with their animal companion. Perhaps they're a wizard who insists on using unnecessarily long-winded spell names - renaming Fireball to "The Inferno of Incendiary Retribution." Or maybe they're a rogue who refuses to steal from anyone wearing yellow because of a traumatic canary incident in their past.

Whatever the quirk, it gives the player an instant handle on who this character is and sets the stage for some memorable roleplay. It's like giving them a ready-made catchphrase or a defining habit they can lean into when they're unsure what to do.

Creating characters on the fly isn't just for emergencies — sometimes, it's exactly what the game needs. Imagine a player shows up late but wants to jump in immediately, or maybe your party adopts an NPC out of nowhere and decides they're a new sidekick. In these cases, improv-building a character keeps the game moving without breaking immersion.

Let's say your players rescue a grumpy blacksmith during a goblin raid, and suddenly they're insisting he join the party. You can quickly spin up a fighter who's more comfortable with an anvil than an ambush, but who's surprisingly deadly with a hammer. A couple of quick stats, a gruff attitude, and a muttered, "I swear I was just here to fix a horseshoe," and you're good to go.

Creating on the fly works best when the stakes are low and the goal is immediate fun. These characters don't need elaborate backstories; they just need to fit the vibe of the moment. And who knows? That quick-build bard who joined because they "got lost on the way to a gig" might end up being someone's favorite character. Sometimes, spontaneity leads to the best stories.

So, whether you're crafting characters with the meticulous care of a master artisan or slapping them together like a roadside mechanic fixing a flat, the key is to make them feel alive and ready for adventure. Give them a goal, a quirk, and enough personality to spark curiosity. Because at the end of the day, no one remembers the perfectly optimized stats — they remember the rogue who refused to steal from yellow-wearers or the wizard whose spell names sounded like Victorian poetry.

Balancing Story and Mechanics When Creating Characters

As you're making these custom characters, remember that balance is key. Use existing classes and races as your guideposts, but don't be afraid to tweak things a little to make the character more interesting or to fit the player's personality. Maybe you swap out a skill proficiency for something more flavorful or give them a minor magic item that ties into their backstory. Just keep it fair, and make sure whatever you give to one character doesn't make the others feel like they're missing out.

Balance isn't just about making sure your character isn't a walking doom cannon; it's about making their mechanics sing in harmony with their story. Let's say you've got a player who wants to be a cursed knight bound to a sentient, shadow-forged blade.

The story screams dark power with a cost, so let the mechanics echo that tension. Sure, give them the ability to channel their blade's malevolent energy for devastating attacks - but tie it to a risk. Maybe every time they unleash that power, they roll a d20, and on a 1, the blade takes control for a round, turning on friend and foe alike.

Now, the player has a deliciously dangerous tool, and every swing feels like a gamble. The character's struggle isn't just narrative fluff; it's baked right into the gameplay. When the mechanics and story reinforce each other like this, every moment becomes a high-stakes dance with destiny. And deep within lies the real magic.

Another handy tip: consider how the character might naturally fit into the campaign. It can be daunting for a new player to figure out why their character is here, in this tavern, agreeing to hunt down a pack of ogres with a bunch of strangers. By giving them a built-in reason - a connection to another character, a personal grudge against ogres, or even just "my patron told me this was important, and I'm not allowed to ask why" - you make it easier for them to jump right into the action. Plus, it saves you from those awkward, "uh, I guess you're just... here now?" moments.

Remember, even though you're creating these characters for your players, you still want to give them ownership. Let them tweak things once they're comfortable - maybe they decide their character's alignment shifts over time, or they want to take a different feat at the next level up.

The point of starting them off with a pre-made character isn't to take away their agency; it's to give them a launching pad, something they can use to dive into the game without getting bogged down by choice paralysis. After all, the faster they can start rolling dice, the sooner everyone can get to the really important part: setting goblins on fire, making terrible puns, and becoming emotionally attached to a sentient sword named Steve.

So, pre-make a few characters, tailor them as best you can, and be ready to adjust on the fly. Your players will thank you for it, and you'll thank yourself when the game gets rolling smoothly without any of those character-creation growing pains.

Steal Like a Thief - You Can Get Away with It

Ah, yes, the old adage: good artists borrow, great artists steal, which I briefly mentioned in the last book, but will repeat here because, dear DMs, it's time to free yourself from the shackles of originality. It's overrated. If you think that every famous creator out there is concocting completely unique ideas from scratch, let me introduce you to the concept of inspiration, which is a nice way of saying, "I borrowed (cough cough, stole) this from somewhere else, but I made it cool in my own way."

And if you are sitting here, staring at that open notebook, feeling the weight of trying to come up with something entirely new, let me tell you something: stop. If there is something you love from your favorite movie, book, game, anime, or whatever else you're into - steal it. Yes, I mean shamelessly hijack it.

Want to create an adventure about a ring that has to be thrown into a volcano while a bunch of broody warriors argue about who gets to carry it? Have at it. Think a Death Star-style superweapon would bring a little pizzazz to your campaign? Slap that bad boy right in there. Because here is the dirty truth: your players don't care where the idea came from. They care about the experience they have with it, and that experience is entirely yours to craft.

In this context, it's really okay to steal because whatever drew you to that piece of media is bound to be something with good execution. Like, there is a reason why it worked, you know?

Now, before any lawyers kick down my door, let me clarify: I'm talking about in-house fun here - the kind of homebrew that never leaves your gaming table and exists purely for your group's chaos-fueled enjoyment. If you're crafting content for your personal game nights and not planning to slap a price tag on it or sneak it onto a store shelf, you've got free rein to mix, match, and mash up whatever cool ideas spark joy.

Want to run a treasure-hunting campaign set in the lush, bioluminescent world of Avatar (yes, the blue-people one) and give your players lightsabers for slicing through alien foliage and angry mech suits? Who's going to stop you? Certainly not the copyright police when it's all for the sacred cause of your group's ridiculous amusement.

The beauty of stealing from your favorite media is that it's familiar and exciting - both for you and your players. You love it, which means you're going to be enthusiastic about bringing it into your game, and that enthusiasm is contagious. Plus, it's a great shortcut for explaining things to your players. It sure beats having to create the whole world from scratch, too. If your players are already familiar with the basics of your world because it's based on Pokemon or The Witcher, that's less time used for lore dumping and more time spent on awesome action and drama.

But the trick to borrowing is to make it yours. Change enough so that it feels fresh, even if you're lifting the core idea. Take Star Wars, for instance. Maybe you love the concept of Jedi, but instead of a galaxy-wide mystical order, you make them a secret sect of warriors bound by ancient oaths in one kingdom trying to maintain balance in their failing monarchy. Now you've got something new yet something recognizable enough that the players can latch onto it, but with its own unique twist that makes it feel like it belongs in your world. It's like remixing a song you love:

the core elements remain, but you put your own spin on the track.

And it doesn't have to be huge concepts, either. You can take much smaller things and borrow those, like an archetype of character, a setting, or even just a vibe. Think of your favorite villains. Is there some character that you really love to hate, like Azula from Avatar (the wind one this time) or Killmonger from Black Panther? You can absolutely lift the best parts of those characters - the ruthlessness, the motivation, the complicated morality - and inject that right into the veins of your villain. Your big bad could be a former ally who's turned against the players because they thought she was dead and left her behind while escaping Horde territory. That kind of complexity makes your story all the richer, and you don't need to reinvent the wheel to get there.

Heck, you can even borrow lines of dialogue if you want. Trust me, when your players hear an NPC shout, "I am inevitable! " right before they snap their fingers, they're not going to say, "Hey, isn't that from Avengers? " They're going to think, "Oh no, something terrible is about to happen," and they're going to be on the edge of their seats.

And isn't that the point? The drama, the tension, the excitement - all of that is real, even if the words themselves came from someone else's script. And the best part about this whole stealing thing is that it's totally liberating. You're no longer shackled by the fear that your idea isn't original enough or that someone will think that you copied something.

Spoiler alert: everyone copies something. Every hero, every villain, every plot twist has been done in a hundred different ways. What makes it unique is how you use it.

It's your players, your story, your world. You take the raw material - be it from a blockbuster movie or a cult classic - and shape it into something that will make your players remember your game for years to come.

Now go ahead, borrow that trope-defining plotline, that character with their tragic backstory, or that villain and their nefarious plot. Make it your own, make it fun, and besides, who worries about being original - just worry about making sure everyone has a blast. Because at the end of the day, your players will remember one thing: that amazing adventure they had with it. And that is what really counts.

Conclusion: The Edge of the Known World

You've made it to the end, where the map frays at the edges, and the carefully planned pathways give way to wild, uncharted territory. This is the threshold where preparation meets spontaneity. Where the ink runs out and pure imagination takes over. Because here's the truth: no matter how detailed your world, how polished your lore, or how meticulously crafted your homebrew, the real magic of

Dungeon Mastering lives in the space between what you've planned and what your players decide to do with it.

Worldbuilding isn't about rigid boundaries. It's about creating a landscape that can hold the weight of a thousand unexpected decisions and still keep standing. It's about offering just enough structure to give your players something solid to leap from, and just enough flexibility to let them land wherever their wild ideas take them. You might sculpt intricate political intrigues or design sprawling deserts of endless peril, but all it takes is one rogue's sideways grin or a wizard's ill-timed spell for your careful plans to unravel - and that's where the fun really begins.

Homebrewing, too, thrives on this delicate balancing act of intention and improvisation. You might craft a magic sword imbued with the gravitas of ancient prophecy, only for your players to use it to butter toast because they couldn't find a knife. Or you invent a tragic NPC with a backstory that took you three days to write, and your players only love him because he sneezes like a kitten. These aren't derailments; they're opportunities. Your world breathes, evolves, and thrives because of the chaos your players inject into it. Let them be the unpredictable heart that pumps life into your creations.

Remember, no matter how grand or intricate your plans, the most vivid worlds are the ones your players shape with their choices. They'll remember the time their half-baked scheme actually worked, that NPC they adopted on a whim, or the dungeon they refused to enter because it smelled weird. Let their actions leave footprints in the world as they feel the weight of their decisions and the ripple effects of their missteps and victories. Often, the stories that stick aren't the ones you force into place, but instead the ones that spread naturally, like a drop of ink into water.

So, as you step away from the safety of preparation and into the unknown of active play, trust your instincts and embrace the chaos. When the map runs out, and the plan goes sideways, don't panic - improvise. That's where the real magic happens. After all, your players aren't here to marvel at a world you've built; they're here to live in it. And when they do, the adventure becomes something bigger, something messier, something unforgettable.

Chapter 2:
Creating Longer Campaigns

Most people dive into video games for the thrill of a good journey - the grind of leveling up, the joy of watching their character grow, and, of course, the sweet, sweet satisfaction of finally taking down that final boss who's been laughing in their faces for weeks. Tabletop RPGs may have given rise to video games, but that craving for an epic, hard-won adventure is universal.

The same drive that keeps gamers glued to their screens is what fuels your players at the table. They want to forge stories, survive challenges, and feel like they've conquered something bigger than themselves. And the best part? You're the architect of that experience, the puppet master behind the curtain, the one who builds the world they'll struggle through, and the villain who'll loom over them until the final, climactic showdown. It's a lot of pressure, sure, but

71 | *Creating Longer Campaigns*

if you nail it, you won't just be running a game - you'll be creating legends.

Of course, unlike a video game, there's no handy-dandy save point or a convenient "Restart from Last Checkpoint" button if things go sideways. Your campaign is more like an intricately crafted Jenga tower - one that's built on character arcs, plot twists, and the tenuous balance between player excitement and the ever-present threat of absolute chaos.

There are no scripted moments that always happen the same way for every player - it's just you, a bunch of players who will definitely try to seduce the dragon, and a story that's got to span more than just a one-off adventure. So, how do you create something that lasts? Something that makes your players want to keep coming back, even after they've just been ambushed for the third time in a row by goblins that refuse to die like good, respectful goblins should?

Creating a longer campaign is all about designing for longevity. It's not enough to have a killer hook at the beginning; you need the kind of narrative depth that can carry your players across months (or even years) of gameplay without them feeling like they're stuck in a Groundhog Day reboot.

We're talking about a campaign that's got layers - like an onion, or Shrek, or parfaits; everybody likes parfaits. You need hooks that keep your players invested, twists that genuinely surprise them (not the M. Night Shyamalan kind that everyone will see a mile away and groan at), and climaxes that make them feel like the heroes they've always dreamed of being.

That's just the big picture, though. To really hit that long campaign sweet spot, you're going to need to master the art of the act break - those moments where your campaign shifts gears, giving your players that breath of fresh air before plunging them into even deeper trouble. You might even want to throw in a fake climax or two because nothing says "I'm a brilliant Dungeon Master" quite like making your players think they've reached the final showdown... only for them to discover that, plot twist, it was just the warm-up for the real nightmare that's about to begin.

But it's not all about plot structure and pacing. No, no, no - long campaigns thrive on unforgettable NPCs, those key characters with whom your players will form deep connections (or deep-seated grudges against).

Think of these NPCs as your campaign's cast of recurring guest stars - the Loki to your Thor, the Gollum to your Frodo, or just Dobby the house-elf. These story-important NPCs need real backgrounds, real motivations, and a purpose that ties them intrinsically to the plot. They shouldn't just exist to serve tea (herbal) or serve tea (verbal) - they need to be the characters who make your players sit up and say, "It was the *butler*?"

It's always the butler!

Executing a great campaign design also comes down to how you weave the threads of the larger narrative into each individual session. This is about ensuring that every single game night serves a purpose, contributing to the bigger picture in some meaningful way.

You want those one-off sessions that feel like quirky side quests to still loop back to the main plot eventually - think of it like an episode of *Avatar: The Last Airbender*. Sure, sometimes we're just helping a village fight off the local firebender bullies, but you know, deep down, that it's all building to something greater. Each session should keep moving the players toward that climactic moment, with enough twists and detours to keep them guessing the whole way.

Let's not forget about the pacing. Keeping a longer campaign fresh and exciting is a bit like keeping a *Game of Thrones* viewer interested: it's all about the hooks and the twists. You need to hit them with a good hook at the start of each session - something that connects personally to the characters or pushes the plot forward in a way they just can't ignore.

And when things start to feel a little too comfortable, it's time to bring out the shock value - those game-changing twists that throw everything your players thought they knew out the window. Maybe their seemingly trustworthy guide was secretly the villain all along, or maybe that ancient artifact they've been trying to destroy is actually just Doop Doop, the seemingly evil but actually just annoying broom. The point is, if your players aren't sitting on the edge of their seats, wondering what's coming next, you're not doing it right.

This chapter is about taking your players on a journey that isn't just epic - the kind of journey they'll be talking about long after the final die roll. It's about the big picture, the unforgettable NPCs, and the perfectly timed twists that make the story sing. If done well, your players won't just be in it for the final boss - they'll be in it for every glorious, gut-wrenching, laughter-filled moment leading up to it. And hey, if they end up still trying to seduce that villain, at least now you'll have the tools to make that awkward dinner date part of the grand design.

Going into the rest of this chapter (as well as the rest of this book), I will teach you *everything* I know, but will act like you're Jon Snow, and you know nothing. Now, I *know* that isn't true and that you know things (and drink wine?). But, inevitably, there will be things you *do* know, so use those sections as a refresher and keep on reading because there's always something new waiting ahead. Just focus on what's new to you and trust me - you'll become the expert Dungeon Master you always wanted to be.

Designing for Longevity

What's the best way to keep a campaign going for years? Design it that way in the first place. Seriously, you're rarely going to get to run a full-length campaign if that wasn't the plan from the get go. In a way, campaign design is similar to session design - relying on hooks, twists, and satisfying resolutions.

When designing a campaign, you might find yourself doing a surprising amount of writing - which can at times feel discouraging. The secret is to keep at it, give your players agency, and find a way to enjoy the process yourself. But I'm getting ahead of myself.

Running a game for your players is just an extension of your creative writing skillset. The core principles are the same. The only real difference is that instead of crafting a story on your own, you're balancing a live, collaborative narrative with a hefty dose of improvisation. If you can master the art of adapting storytelling techniques on the fly, you'll be well on your way to crafting sessions that keep your players immersed, invested, and eager to see what happens next. The best part? The campaign gets to grow with you, each session you get to be a new and more improved version of yourself. You *can* and should run that huge campaign you've been dreaming of. Get started now, yes, *right* now, and I'll help guide you towards improvement as you go.

The first thing you'll need is a good story. Let's dive into the meat and potatoes of campaign longevity - hooks, twists, and climaxes. You won't believe what hooks I have in store for you; keep reading to find out! See what I did there? No? Well, you're about to.

The Art of a Good Hook

A hook is exactly what it sounds like - it's what catches your players' attention and refuses to let go, like the tentacles of a Kraken wrapping around the hull of a doomed pirate ship. Unlike your average fish, though, a campaign hook doesn't take a mere moment; it's long-lasting and important. It's what keeps your players coming back whenever your schedules magically (and infrequently) align - because, let's be honest, scheduling conflicts are the true Big Bad of TTRPGs.

A campaign hook, unlike the episodic cliffhangers we'll get into later, is about resonance. It's got to hum through the entire campaign, from the first dungeon crawl to the final showdown - it has to be something that can encompass the entire arc.

Imagine your players find an ancient artifact with mysterious powers - one that's clearly important but dangerous. That's a hook that can keep on giving. Where did it come from? Why are there so many factions suddenly after them? Is it evil? And, of course, will anyone ever be foolish enough to put on the Ancient Sombrero of Great Mysterious Power? (Spoiler alert: someone will.)

Take the classic "missing mentor" trope. The party's beloved mentor vanishes without a trace, leaving behind only cryptic clues. Where did they go? Who's behind their disappearance? Are they even still alive, or is this some kind of elaborate test? It's like Obi-Wan Kenobi pulling a disappearing act but with more explosions and maybe a cursed amulet thrown in for good measure.

A great hook is the narrative equivalent of dangling a double-chocolate chip cookie just out of reach - it needs to be irresistible, spark curiosity, and leave your players lunging forward to find out what happens next. It's the bait on your storytelling fishing line, and if you dangle it just right, your players will bite hard and drag themselves right into the plot for you.

First off, the core of any effective hook is the *question*. Not the kind of question that makes your players shrug and mutter, "Cool, whatever," but the kind that ignites the spark of need-to-know curiosity. A good hook doesn't just invite interest; it demands it.

Think of it like stumbling across a locked door in a video game. Your brain immediately screams, "What's behind that door? Why is it locked? And who do I have to beat up to get the key?"

Let's say your players come to a village that has been ravaged by fire. The players may pause momentarily to feel empathy, but if there's no question for them to answer, they'll just move on. Instead, drop a scorched symbol amongst the wreckage - something obscure and forbidding that just feels like it shouldn't be there. Suddenly, their brains are firing off like a detective's conspiracy board: Who burned the village? What does the symbol mean? Are they next? It's no longer just rubble; it's a mystery that needs solving.

Your hook can be as simple or complex as you want, but simplicity often works best for instant engagement. Think of it like the first ten minutes of a mystery show. Does it give you an entire history lesson? No. It slaps you with a juicy, unresolved puzzle: Someone's missing, someone's dead, or someone's hiding something. You don't need the entire plot mapped out - just enough to trigger that itch in your players' minds that won't go away until they scratch it.

In essence, the magic formula for creating a good hook requires you to combine intrigues, stakes, and urgency. Intrigue is the question they need to answer; stakes are the consequences if they ignore it or fail, and urgency is that ticking clock that makes them feel they *must* act now.

Imagine this: A shady courier collapses at the party's feet in a busy marketplace, clutching a sealed letter and gasping, "It's too late... they're already here..." before going limp.

Intrigue? What's in the letter, and who are those mysterious "they"?

Stakes? If they don't open that letter and do something about it, someone (or everyone) might be in serious trouble.

Urgency? If "they" are already here, the clock's ticking faster than a Fred Jones in a trap-filled mansion.

Hooks work best when they connect to your players' motivations or backstories. This is where you sprinkle in a little personalization. If you know your rogue is obsessed with lost artifacts, toss a clue to find an ancient relic into their lap. If your barbarian is searching for their missing clan, dangle a lead that points straight to their homeland. The hook shouldn't just snag their attention - it should 'hook' into who they are.

Let me first touch on framing because how you present your plotline is half the battle. Anyone can say, "Hey, there's a treasure map, wanna follow it?" But if the players find that map sewn into the lining of a murdered noble's cloak, with a bloody handprint smeared across it and a cryptic note that says, "Don't let him find it first..." suddenly, it's not just a map. It's a thrill ride waiting to happen. It's the difference between a casual, "Hey, wanna play?" and a desperate, "You have to help me before it's too late!"

Of course, not every hook needs to be life-or-death. Sometimes, the best hooks are just plain weird. An entire village where no one remembers who they are. A talking cat that offers a riddle in exchange for a favor. A door that appears in the middle of a field, unattached to any building. The sheer oddity of it will gnaw at their curiosity like a beaver on a log. If they don't investigate, it'll bug them forever.

Now, you might be thinking, "What if my players don't take the bait?" Well, that's the beauty of a well-crafted hook - it doesn't rely on railroading. If they ignore one, you've got another up your sleeve. Maybe they passed on the dying courier's letter, but then a mysterious figure starts to follow them. Maybe they ignore the talking cat, but later, they find a note signed with a paw print. Hooks are like plot ninjas: if one misses, another is waiting to pounce.

Finally, let the players get caught on your hook themselves. Drop enough information to tease the question but leave the resolution to them. Your job isn't to drag them along - it's to make the path so intriguing that they choose to run down it. They should feel like they've stumbled into a puzzle box and now have to figure out how to open it, not because you said so, but because they can't help themselves.

So, next time you're setting up your session, think of that tantalizing question, dangle it with just the right mix of intrigue, stakes, and urgency, and watch your players sink their teeth in. Just remember: the best hooks leave your party desperate for answers and maybe, just maybe, questioning their life choices as they chase down a talking cat through a burning village. If that isn't what TTRPGs are all about, then why are we even here... just to suffer?

Now, compare campaign hooks to individual or session hooks. These are more like a delicious breadcrumb that leads to the next piece of the pie - they are the same little twists you throw in at the end of a *Dragon Ball Z* episode.

Your players have defeated the bandits and reclaimed the stolen idol, only to find out it was a decoy. Cue surprised Pikachu faces. They need to know what happens next. Where's the real idol? What else are these bandits hiding? A session hook leads directly into the next adventure - it's a constant feed of intrigue that keeps the players moving but isn't necessarily the driving force of the whole campaign.

The secret to keeping a campaign alive is to use these hooks - both campaign-wide and session-based - to weave a compelling narrative tapestry. Good hooks make your players invested. It's that investment that turns a random Tuesday evening dice fest into an unforgettable epic.

Twist of Fate

Twists are what give a narrative tapestry its texture. These are the moments when everything the players thought they knew gets turned upside down. Twists are why the true villain wasn't the mayor, it was the butler all along, and why the benevolent king the party was serving was secretly an ancient dragon in disguise.

A good twist isn't just a "gotcha" moment - it's a revelation that changes the stakes and forces the players to reevaluate their entire strategy. A good twist, much like in cinema or literature, should feel both surprising and inevitable. Think of *The Sixth Sense* where you suddenly realize Bruce Willis has been dead the entire time, or *Fight Club,* when you find out that Tyler Durden isn't real.

The key is laying the groundwork early. Imagine you're planting seeds in the fertile chaos of your campaign world. These seeds are tiny hints - cryptic remarks from NPCs, strange symbols carved into ancient ruins, or that one detail the players shrugged off as background fluff because they were too busy looting everything that wasn't nailed down. You don't need to make these hints scream, "TWIST INCOMING!" In fact, subtlety is your best friend here. Let them blend seamlessly into the story, hiding in plain sight. The players should notice them, but also *not* notice them, you know? Like background music in a tavern - it's there, it adds atmosphere, but it doesn't demand attention.

Then, when you spring the twist, those quiet little details snap into focus like the final piece of a puzzle slotting into place. That grumpy blacksmith who's been feeding the party info? Turns out he's the brother of the Big Bad they've been hunting. The mysterious sword they found two towns ago? Oh, it's not just enchanted - it's cursed, and now they're the pawn in an ancient prophecy they accidentally walked into.

83 | *Creating Longer Campaigns*

The players didn't stumble onto these revelations; they earned them through their journey. The twist isn't some random lightning bolt; it's the storm they've been building towards all along.

In these integral moments, the last thing you want is to drop a twist out of nowhere like a dragon swooping in to solve a plot hole you didn't know how to fix. Nothing breaks immersion faster than a twist that feels like it was crammed in because you painted yourself into a narrative corner. Your players need to feel like the twist was always part of the plan, even if you cooked it up three seconds ago while pretending to check your notes.

One way to make sure your twist is woven into the campaign's fabric is to let your players' actions steer the story. Maybe they decide to trust the shady scholar instead of the kindly village elder. Great! Let that choice sow the seeds of the twist. Perhaps the scholar's been using them to uncover forbidden knowledge all along. The twist grows naturally from their decisions, and when the reveal hits, they can't complain about you railroading them - they drove right into that mess themselves.

When it comes to twists, you *have to* pace yourself. Twists shouldn't feel like you're yanking the rug out from under them every other session. You need to build up anticipation and let the tension simmer like a pot of stew on a low boil. Drop a hint here and a clue there. Let them chase red herrings or misinterpret things wildly (because, let's be honest, they will). Then, when the moment is right - BAM! The twist lands and it feels like a series of dominoes cascading into one another. The best part? The players realize they've been headed toward this all along.

A good twist isn't just about the initial shocked faces and trembling knees - it's about the butterfly effect it sends throughout the rest of the campaign. Maybe the twist reveals a hidden enemy they didn't know they had, or maybe an ally they trusted becomes suspect. The aftermath of a twist is where the real magic happens - watching your players scramble to adjust their plans, reassess their relationships, and desperately try to patch together a new strategy. That's where you get those juicy, memorable moments that become the stuff of campaign legend.

So, take the time to weave your twists carefully, let them sprout from the story naturally, and watch your players' faces light up (or go pale) when the trap finally snaps shut. Because when a twist hits just right, it's not just a game - it's a moment. And moments like that? They're why we roll the dice in the first place.

The key is to build upon those moments until they become a perfectly satisfying resolution. You made them ask questions, spring into action, and yearn to save the day. Then, you threw twists in their plans, but they still persevered. Well, now is the time to give them a satisfying resolution.

Resolution

What ties it all together is the climax, or the resolution. The moment when all the tension you've built finally snaps like an overstretched rubber band. Every campaign worth its salt needs a proper climax - that final, nail-biting showdown that feels earned.

It's the moment when Frodo finally reaches Mount Doom, when Harry faces off against Voldemort, or when Marty McFly has to get the DeLorean up to 88 mph at the exact moment the lightning strikes the clock. Without a climax, all those hooks and twists would just be a bunch of teases with no payoff. A good climax gives your players a sense of accomplishment, the feeling that all their decisions and dice rolls meant something.

Picture the party storming the tower of the dark sorcerer who has been the source of all their troubles. They've fought their way through traps, minions, and perhaps even a brainwashed ally. The sorcerer stands at the top, ready to complete a ritual that will plunge the world into eternal darkness.

This is it. The moment your players have been inching toward for months - the grand crescendo, the showdown that's been teased, hinted at, and looms over them like a dark storm cloud full of lightning and poor life choices. The stakes are sky-high, and every choice, every spell, every "Are you sure you want to do that?" matters.

This isn't just another fight; this is The Fight - the culmination of their blood, sweat, and emotionally questionable decision-making. If you do it right, this climax becomes the stuff of legends. If you do it wrong, well... let's just say you don't want your campaign's ending to be the next *Mass Effect 3*.

To avoid that dreaded reaction, your climax needs to hit those sweet, cathartic beats your players have been craving. They should feel the weight of everything that came before - the victories, the heartbreaks, the spectacular failures that ended in facepalms and existential dread. When the dust settles, they should be able to look back and go, "Yes, it was all worth it." Every step on that perilous road led them here, and it needs to feel like it. This isn't the time for half-baked finales or vague, hand-wavy resolutions. This is where you tie those threads together, knot them into a glorious tapestry, and slam it onto the table with a flourish.

If you want to have a good payoff, let your players' choices matter in the climax. If the rogue saved that shady informant three sessions ago, let that informant show up with a crucial piece of intel or an escape route when things begin to look bleak. If the barbarian swore a blood oath of vengeance, let this be the moment where that promise is fulfilled in a blaze of glorious fury. This is where all those little callbacks and consequences come home to roost. The players need to see their journey reflected in this finale - their actions shaping the climax.

A satisfying resolution isn't just about the fight; it's also about the fallout. Give your players a moment after the dust settles to soak it all in. Maybe they're standing on the battlefield, panting and victorious, watching the sun rise on a new world they helped save (or helped doom, depending on how things shook out).

Ultimately, delivering a satisfying resolution is about respecting the journey and honoring the stakes. Give your players closure, throw in enough twists to keep them on their toes, and cap it off with a moment that makes them lean back, smile, and say, "That was epic." And hey, if they're still talking about it months later, you know you've done it right.

The end doesn't have to be predictable, either. Sure, they should get the payoff they've worked towards, but sprinkle in just enough surprises to keep them gripping their dice and whispering, "Oh no, oh no, oh no, oh YEAH!" like a caffeinated Kool-Aid Man. If they're heading toward the Big Bad with the confidence of a plot-armored anime protagonist, have the villain reveal a secret weapon, a hidden ally, or — plot twist — they weren't even the real villain. Surprise, you've been chasing a puppet! Now, the real mastermind steps out of the shadows, and suddenly, that final battle just got a lot spicier.

Fake Climax

Fake climaxes (otherwise known as two-part climaxes) are the rollercoaster moments before the real drop. It's when the players think they're about to face the final villain, only to find out it was actually just a powerful minion - or that the real mastermind has been two steps ahead of them the entire time.

It's like playing a video game, thinking you're about to face the ultimate big bad, only to find out that there's actually an even bigger cosmic horror lurking in the background. A well-crafted fake climax is like a perfectly executed jump scare that doesn't just end with a "gotcha! " but kicks off an even more intense sequence. The power of a fake climax in a TTRPG campaign allows your players to feel the rush of an almost-victory while planting the seeds for an even greater threat.

It's a rollercoaster that careens down its steepest, longest drop, only to suddenly reverse back up it to rush down the other side *backward*. Let's say your players have spent months tracking down the evil necromancer who's been plaguing the kingdom. They confront him, there's an epic battle, spells flying, swords clashing, and they finally defeat him. Cue the cheers, the victory poses, and the rogue making a dramatic hair flip.

But wait!

As the necromancer crumples, his body dissipates into a cloud of black smoke, and with a chilling voice, he utters his final words, "I was but a pawn." The true enemy then appears - the lich who built this necromancer - and he is fully aware of the party's existence, beginning to hunt them. The players thought they were finished but instead find they've only just scratched the surface. That's a fake climax done right: it shifts the stakes, broadens the scope, and makes the journey feel far more dangerous and grand.

To pull this off effectively, make sure the fake climax feels real. Let your players go all in - give them dramatic stakes, an emotional payoff, and enough tension to make them sweat. The encounter should be satisfying in its own right, not just a placeholder. If the players feel cheated or like their effort was pointless, you've missed the mark. The fake climax should close one chapter of the story while seamlessly opening another.

Use foreshadowing to hint that all may not be as it seems. Perhaps the villain they're fighting drops cryptic hints during combat. Maybe there are clues along the way - ancient texts, NPCs who warn of something worse, or magical artifacts that react strangely during the battle. These subtle signals set up the twist without giving it away completely, making the reveal feel earned rather than random.

But remember: fake climaxes are like spicy food. A little bit makes everything more exciting but add too much, and everyone feels duped and queasy. If every major confrontation turns out to be a bait-and-switch, your players will lose trust in the narrative. Instead of feeling thrilled, they'll start second-guessing every encounter, like paranoid detectives in a bad mystery novel. When you do pull the rug out, make sure there's something even juicier beneath it — a twist that feels like it was worth the deception.

In the end, a fake climax isn't about tricking your players - it's about giving them a story that keeps evolving, expanding, and surprising them. Done right, it will make the real climax hit with the force of a meteor strike, leaving your players breathless, exhilarated, and maybe just a little scared of what you'll throw at them next.

If you want to achieve that glorious dream of running a level one to level twenty campaign, you've got to prepare for the long haul. We're talking years of twists, turns, and table-flipping drama, so you'll need something (other than snacks) to keep your players fueled and fired up along the way. The main plot can't wrap up five sessions in, but that doesn't mean they should be stuck in a perpetual slog. Throw them a bone, give them victories that feel like endings - because nothing keeps a campaign thriving like the perfectly timed satisfaction of an act break.

Act Breaks

Let's talk about act breaks. Campaigns, like any good stage play, can benefit from being broken into acts. Each act is a major phase in the storyline, usually culminating in a significant revelation or battle - sort of like your TV season finale.

Within each act, you have the hooks, twists, and smaller climaxes that lead to the big moment at the end. Act breaks are great opportunities for character development, allowing players to regroup, reassess, and evolve their relationships and goals. It's just like a play - the curtain falls, the scene changes and everyone gets a moment to breathe before the next round of drama begins. Think of it like a filler episode of your favorite TV show. Like when *One Piece* blesses us with a single episode of filler between two ninety-five episode arcs.

Think of the original Star Wars trilogy's structure. A New Hope wraps up with a satisfying act break: the Death Star goes boom, the heroes bask in glory, and for one shining moment, the galaxy dares to hope. But The Empire Strikes Back flips the table, dropping a seismic twist that shatters the status quo and leaves everyone dangling on the edge of despair. Sure, the first movie could stand alone, but Empire drags you toward a resolution you need to see. That's the itch you want to plant in your players' brains - a burning drive to know what's next, a promise that the story hasn't peaked, and the tantalizing sense that the real payoff is still on the horizon.

Writing and theater give us fantastic lessons for TTRPG campaigns. And trust me, as someone with a *incredibly* useful theater degree I *totally* don't regret paying for, I would know. The use of acts, climaxes, and hooks all serve to create pacing that feels natural and keeps players engaged. Remember, the goal isn't just to tell a story - it's to tell a story that matters. Give them a hook they can't resist, twists they'll never see coming, and a climax that leaves them cheering (or sobbing, depending on your particular brand of DMing).

And when all else fails, just add a dragon. Because, let's be honest, dragons make everything better. Or, if you're feeling spicy, a lich. Because nothing says, "We're in the endgame now," quite like an undead sorcerer with a god complex.

To keep your campaign rolling with those epic highs and gut-punch twists, you -need more than just a solid structure - you need characters who matter. And I'm not talking about your run-of-the-mill quest-givers or shopkeepers with a bad attitude. No, I'm talking about the NPCs who stick in your players' minds, the ones who turn plot points into emotional rollercoasters. What's coming next involves some of the most powerful tools in your storytelling arsenal.

Story-important NPCs

You've already got the basics of NPC creation down - quirky shopkeepers, brooding mercenaries, and at least one bard with questionable life choices. But now it's time to step up and create the NPCs who really matter. These are the linchpins of your story, the ones who make your plot feel like more than just a series of events.

It's in creating story-important NPCs that you really level up as a Dungeon Master. These characters aren't just there to fill space or hand out quests; they're the heartbeat of your narrative. They're the ones who forge emotional connections with your players, who leave scars - literally or metaphorically - and who make your world feel alive. These are the NPCs your players will laugh about, cry over, or rage against long after the campaign ends. They're the characters who steal the spotlight in fan art, memes, and heated debates over whether or not they deserved what happened to them. In short, these NPCs are what make your game unforgettable.

We've all experienced an NPC who became a staple of the campaign in one way or another. Maybe the party found them really useful in combat and kept them around. Maybe they had an affinity for poorly-timed puns, and the party needed comic relief. Whatever the reason, let's explore how to craft these memorable characters on purpose and not just with a happy little accident.

I won't sugarcoat it: forging these kinds of NPCs is no simple alchemy. It's not just a matter of conjuring a name, whispering a half-baked purpose into the ether, and sprinkling on a quirky accent like it's fairy dust (though, let's be honest, a well-timed posh accent or gravelly growl can work wonders).

To make a story-important NPC that resonates, you've got to go deeper. You've got to create characters with layered backstories, compelling motivations, and enough personality to stand out from the sea of tavernkeepers and faceless shopkeepers the party's been rolling past. These NPCs don't just exist in your world; they shape it, sometimes for the better and sometimes for pure evil.

Every great story-important NPC needs a reason to exist. And no, "I needed someone to give the party their next quest" isn't good enough. These sorts of NPCs aren't just plot devices - they're characters unto themselves.

They have histories, motivations, and lives that don't revolve around the players - but they inevitably get entangled with the party's antics. Ask yourself: why is this character here? What shaped them? What do they want? And why do they care about what's happening in the campaign? Once you have these questions answered, you will know how to structure their backstories and give them the right motivation.

Let me tell you about a character from one of my campaigns. Her name was Elira, and she was a high-ranking official in a religious order. For all intents and purposes, she was there to provide the party with information and guidance. But her real story? She'd lost faith in the gods she served after a catastrophic event for which she blamed herself.

Every interaction she had with the party wasn't just to further the plot along; it was an inner struggle between her duty and her own personal doubts. The players, of course, didn't pick up on all that at first, but the subtle cracks in her persona kept them guessing. And when her full story came to light, it hit them like a ton of bricks.

No one's asking you to write a novel for every NPC - your players rarely appreciate your four-hour-long lore monologues anyway (and you know it). But a sprinkle of meaningful backstory goes a long way.

Maybe the once-renowned knight is now a gutter drunk because they failed to protect a royal caravan years ago. Maybe the traveling bard's love ballads hit differently once you realize they're all secretly about the same person who left them heartbroken and penniless.

The point is to give them a reason to be interesting. A one-sentence backstory can do wonders, like: "They lost their entire family in the War of Zunesha," or "They're desperately searching for their long-lost twin." Suddenly, that NPC has weight. They have baggage. And baggage makes things juicy.

Take your garden-variety city guard. Instead of "Unnamed Guard #12 stands at the gate," try this: The guard is a former gladiator who threw a match to save their rival's life. Now, disgraced and demoted to gate duty, they're torn between resentment for their lowly post and pride in doing the honorable thing.

How does this help you? Players who chat them up might learn about the criminal underbelly of the arena or maybe discover the guard's old rival is now working for the local crime lord, setting the stage for a revenge arc. The lesson here is that even a lowly guard can become a narrative spark, prompting side quests, moral decisions, and memorable roleplay moments.

One of the biggest reasons why you would give your story-important character a backstory is to establish their motivations. They are the driving force behind any good NPC. What do they want? What are they willing to do to get it? And how do those goals intersect - or clash - with the party's? The best NPCs aren't static. They've got their own plans and ambitions, which can change as the campaign unfolds.

Let me give you a few examples.

Imagine a thief named Garrik. His initial motivation is simple: survive. He's got debts to pay and enemies gunning for him, and he's willing to cut deals with the party to stay alive. But as the story progresses, maybe Garrik realizes he wants more than just survival. Maybe he wants revenge against the people who put him in this position. Or maybe he finds a cause worth fighting for and becomes a reluctant hero. These shifts are what make Garrik feel dynamic and real instead of like a stand-in waiting for the players to move the plot along.

Another example would be a shady noble who keeps showing up whenever the party stumbles onto ancient ruins. Sure, they offer jobs and gold, but why? Maybe they're trying to impress a secret society, gather enough relics to break a family curse, or just want to look cooler than their snooty cousin at the next noble's ball. Their motivations may evolve: what if they start off wanting treasure but, after seeing the party's courage, decide to champion the party's cause instead? Or maybe they screw the party over once, feel guilty about it, and attempt a heartfelt redemption arc. Here's a not-so-secret secret: heartfelt redemption arcs are pure gold in TTRPGs, turning even the most despised NPCs into tear-jerking favorites and giving your players the satisfaction of helping a villain become something more.

Now, let me regale you with one more NPC I thought up - just to give you an example, of course, totally not because I like bragging about my cool NPCs. I mean, since when do theater kids brag? Imagine, if you will, a merchant named

Thornwick. At first, Thornwick is all business - shady deals and rigged scales. His motive: enough coin to pay off a blackmailer threatening to expose Thornwick's past as a petty thief. However, over time, Thornwick sees the party's kindness and realizes he can't keep living in fear, so he starts leaving cryptic tips for the PCs to help them and maybe even confesses his secret. The players get a compelling NPC who grows before their eyes, while you get the satisfaction of watching them debate if he has earned their trust. The lesson here should be straightforward - changing motives will hook your players emotionally, making every interaction carry weight.

An NPC's motivations can also be a source of tension. Perhaps the party's patron is secretly using them to further their own agenda, or the seemingly loyal ally has a personal vendetta that could jeopardize the group's mission. The conflict between an NPC's goals and the party's goals creates drama, and drama creates memorable moments.

Let's be real: nobody remembers Generic Guard #12 or Shopkeeper Steve. They remember the characters who make an impression, whether it's through their humor, their quirks, or their sheer audacity. Personality is what makes an NPC stand out. It's what turns "that guy at the bar" into a beloved - or distained - fixture of the campaign.

Quirks are an easy way to make NPCs memorable. Maybe the stern mercenary leader has a soft spot for poetry and quotes it at the most inappropriate times. Maybe the village herbalist has an encyclopedic knowledge of plants but insists on explaining everything in riddles. Or maybe the crime lord who rules the underworld with an iron fist is also a devoted parent who leaves every meeting early to tuck their kids into bed. These little details make NPCs feel real and relatable.

A bland NPC is like unseasoned tofu - technically food, but who's excited about it? Throw in a few quirks that matter: a necromancer who runs an orphanage by day, a mercenary who hums lullabies to their sword, or a librarian who can't resist correcting everyone's grammar mid-battle. These details are memorable, but be careful not to turn your NPC into a cartoon. Add depth behind the quirk. Does the librarian correct grammar because of a traumatic past where a misread rune blew up her hometown's bakery? Now we're cooking.

There's a fine line between quirky and caricature. The key is to balance the quirks with depth. Give your NPCs layers to avoid the wretched Flanderization. The snarky bard who loves bad puns? Maybe they're using humor to hide the fact that they're carrying a huge secret. The grizzled warrior who never smiles? Maybe they lost their family and are terrified of forming new connections. Quirks are the spice, but the emotional depth is the true substance.

It's worth pointing out that the best NPCs don't exist in a vacuum. They're tied to the world and, ideally, to the players. Maybe they're a veteran from the same war the party's fighter served in or a scholar who mentored the wizard in their younger days. These connections make the NPC feel personal - like they're part of the party's story rather than an obstacle or helper.

Let's revisit Elira. Her religious order was integral to my initial worldbuilding, and her personal struggles mirrored themes the players were dealing with in the campaign. But she wasn't just tied to the setting - she was tied to the players. One of them, a cleric, shared her doubts about their deity, leading to some incredible roleplay moments. On the flip side, the rogue initially distrusted Elira because he was convinced she was hiding something. These relationships made Elira more than just a quest giver; she was a living, breathing part of the story.

When you attach NPCs to the world, consider their relationships and reputation. Are they loved, hated, or feared? Do they have enemies the party might encounter? What about their relationships with the players? Are they a mentor, a rival, a sibling, a lover? Attachments create investment, and investment creates moments people never forget.

It may seem counterintuitive to say, but great NPCs are also boring. Nobody likes the all-knowing sage who always has the right answer or the unbeatable warrior who never loses. What makes NPCs relatable - and lovable - is their flaws. Let them screw up. Let them be wrong. Let them make decisions that blow up in everyone's faces. Everyone loves a train wreck - just not when it derails your entire campaign.

NPCs are meant to play a supporting role - there to enhance the story *and* the world, but not steal the spotlight. Let your players solve that puzzle, romance the barkeep, or strike the final blow on the big bad while you let the NPC support from the sidelines instead of stealing their thunder.

Hands down, my absolute favorite NPC of all time was a wizard named Ansel. He was brilliant but absent-minded, constantly misplacing his spellbook and forgetting key details. During one particularly tense encounter, he cast a fireball in close quarters, hitting both the enemy and the party. It was a disaster - but it was also hilarious, and the players loved him for it. Flaws make NPCs feel human (or elf, or dwarf, or whatever), and they give players opportunities to step in and save the day... or fail miserably.

Flaws can also be used to create drama. Perhaps the party's patron has a gambling problem and keeps "borrowing" from the adventuring fund. Or the trusted guide is secretly working for the enemy but regrets it. These imperfections make NPCs feel real and keep the players on their toes.

The best NPCs don't fall neatly into categories, though. Sure, some will be clear-cut allies or enemies, but the most interesting ones are the ones that blur the lines. The rival adventurer whose obnoxious tendencies are mistaken for pure evil. The noble who's funding the party's mission but has a few skeletons in their closet. The trusted advisor who's loyal to the crown but thinks the party's methods are dangerous.

And then there are the villains. Great villains aren't just evil for the sake of it - they have reasons, goals, and, dare I say it, a touch of sympathy. Maybe the necromancer raising an undead army is doing so to protect their homeland against an even greater threat. Perhaps the corrupt merchant is funneling his ill-gotten gains into building schools for orphaned children.

The more complex the villainy, the more memorable the confrontation - even to an absurd level. Take Dr. Heinz Doofenshmirtz from *Phineas and Ferb*. He's a supervillain, he's amicably divorced, and he was raised by ocelots. But it doesn't stop there. His evil ambitions only ever stretch as far as taking over the Tri-State area, and he's in a romantically coded hilarious rivalry with a sentient platypus. He's an amazing father, legitimately one of the best cartoon dads in history. His parents favored their other son over him, forcing him to stand outside in the rain dressed as a lawn gnome. *Neither* of them even showed up for his *birth*! (Don't ask me how that works.) But, most importantly - he is a character that never gives up and becomes a good guy in the end. Now, *that's* a complex character that left a mark on Disney kids everywhere.

The most memorable NPCs leave a mark, and that mark often comes in the form of big emotional moments. Perhaps it is the sacrifice of a mentor to save the party. Perhaps it is a trusted ally who was actually the villain. Or maybe it's even the comic relief character stepping up and doing something heroic when the time calls for it.

These moments stick because they feel earned. They're not just there for shock value - they're the result of relationships, conflicts, and stories that have been building up for sessions. When the players gasp, cheer, or scream, "NOOOO!" you know you've done it right.

In essence, creating story-important NPCs is all about creating living characters. They aren't just there to provide exposition or dole-out quests - they're there to challenge, inspire, and connect with the players. When done right, these characters become the heart of the campaign, the characters who make your world unforgettable. Once you've conjured up these unforgettable NPCs, it's time to unleash them into your sessions with the kind of finesse that makes your story sing. Is it singing? Great! Now, let's ensure you have the other tools in your toolbelt needed for a campaign to hit as hard as your NPC's dramatic entrances.

Executing on a Good Design

So, you've got your world built out, your overarching plot poised to pounce, and you've even managed to cook up some NPCs so tasty that your players are salivating at the thought of talking to them (or smiting them, depending on the vibe). That's fantastic.

But now comes the hard part: actually running this thing like the pro you're aspiring to be. Designing the campaign is half the battle; executing it is where the rubber meets the road, the dice hit the table, and the players attempt to seduce the dragon... again.

Think of your campaign as a grand machine, all gears and cogs elegantly (or haphazardly) arranged. It's not enough to wind it up at the start and hope it keeps ticking away. You need to regularly add oil (fresh challenges), tighten screws (clarify objectives), and occasionally hit it with a wrench until it starts working again (throw in a wild surprise) to keep your players engaged.

Every session should have a purpose, whether that's moving the main plot forward, exploring a character's backstory, or introducing a bizarre subplot where the party's rogue adopts a talking cat that swears it's a cursed prince.

Let's say the party's main objective is to prevent a looming war between two kingdoms. They've made progress: brokered a fragile truce, exposed a spy in the royal council, and earned the trust of a skeptical queen. Great! But if you take too long to show them the next step or fail to introduce new complications, they'll get restless.

After that diplomatic breakthrough, consider introducing a rumor that power hungry monarchs are sabotaging peace talks behind the scenes. Suddenly, the players have something tangible to chase, a time-sensitive puzzle to solve, and a renewed sense of urgency. The lesson here is simple: never let your players' momentum stagnate; give them fresh leads and evolving stakes to keep them invested.

You can plan the most elaborate storyline this side of Middle-Earth. Still, your players will inevitably say, "Actually, we want to detour to this creepy lighthouse we spotted a few sessions ago," or "We're going to ignore the dire warnings and throw a beach party - suck on that, prophecy!"

Let me make this clear - this is a feature, not a bug. Lean into their choices. Let them feel the weight of their decisions. When you respond organically to their actions - rewarding clever thinking, punishing reckless leaps of faith, and embracing their shenanigans - they'll realize they're not just spectators in your story. They're co-authors.

Imagine your players stumble upon a mysterious map that isn't part of your main plot. They spend the next hour debating whether to follow it to "The Golden Clam" marked on the coast. You didn't expect this, but you roll with it.

Maybe The Golden Clam is an old tavern rumored to hold secret pirate treasure. Or maybe it's a cult meeting spot cleverly disguised as a seafood joint. Either way, when the party arrives and you present a fun mini-arc - complete with suspicious sailors, lost pearls, and a riddle-spouting octopus bartender - they'll feel like their curiosity matters. The lesson: give players room to roam, and they'll love you for making their detours meaningful.

Think of a single game session like an episode of your favorite TV show. It needs a hook (a reason why they should care), rising tension (to complicate the plot), and some form of payoff (a big reveal, epic fight, or hilarious social encounter).

Even if the main campaign arc is huge and far from completion, each session should feel like it accomplished something. If a session ends and your players go, "Well, that happened," without any excitement or lingering questions, you've missed a golden opportunity. Don't be afraid to shuffle scenes around or introduce a late-session twist if things feel too flat.

Let's say you notice mid-session that the players are getting a bit bored slogging through the swamp in search of the rumored Hag of the Marshes. They're rolling survival checks, and chatting amongst themselves about their favorite cat videos. Now we all love a good cat video, but what should you do? The energy is dipping!

107 | Creating Longer Campaigns

Well, it's time to spice it up. Maybe they stumble across a stranded Fey courier with a package they refuse to open. Or maybe they find an abandoned hut with a talking mushroom that's actually the Hag's familiar, taunting them with riddles. Now, the session has gone from "swamp slog" to "intriguing mystery."

By the end of the session, even if they haven't reached the Hag's lair yet, they've got new intel, a quirky NPC ally, or at least a good laugh from that feisty fungus. The lesson is not to be afraid to shake things up if the session drags - do it well and your players will thank you.

You can also keep your players engaged by throwing them a few trinkets here and there - as practical rewards.

Don't just hand out magic items and gold like they're stale candy left over from last Halloween. Give out loot and bonuses that tie into the characters' stories or the campaign's themes. If your ranger is mourning the loss of their ancestral forest, maybe they find seeds from a long-extinct tree they can nurture back to life. If your warlock struggles with their pact, consider awarding them a cryptic prophecy that hints at freeing themselves from their patron's grasp. These aren't just rewards - they're plot hooks that deepen the narrative.

Remember those amazing NPCs you designed? Don't leave them static. Have them learn from the party's actions, grow as individuals, and challenge the party's assumptions.

And then, figure out a way to incorporate that character development into the larger campaign arc.

If the players help a timid scholar overcome their fear of the undead, maybe that scholar becomes braver and more assertive - maybe they even join a monster-hunting guild and offer new quests down the line. If the players disappoint their stern mentor, have the mentor's attitude shift, their guidance dry up, or their trust start to wane until the party earns it back. A dynamic world means no one is stuck reading from the same script session after session.

Obviously, you should apply this advice to players' character development as well. Sure, you might've planned out some other stories, but figure out a way to adapt if a player unexpectedly decides they're more interested in becoming a master intestine knitter. That one might be tough, but you have enough creativity. I believe in you.

Your campaign's epic scope is impressive, but sometimes you need to drill down into the small stuff - an intense one-on-one conversation or a tense social gathering where the rogue tries to bluff a noble. Other times, you're zooming out and montaging travel scenes, skipping over uneventful stretches, or fast-forwarding through the merchant negotiations to keep the story moving. Learning when to spotlight details and when to fade to black is a skill that keeps the game flowing smoothly and preventing the small, unimportant things from stealing center stage.

Let's say the party embarks on a two-week journey across open plains. If nothing interesting happens, montage it: "After days of quiet travel, you pass rolling hills, chat about your hometowns, and share some questionable jerky." But later, when they finally reach the haunted keep, zoom in close on their first cautious steps inside, the eerie creak of old beams and the dusty tapestries hinting at dark secrets.

The main point here is to control the pacing and highlight what matters without wasting time on what doesn't. This 'zoom-in/zoom-out' technique is probably my favorite way of controlling the pace of the story, as well as the pace of the session. Very few players want a narration of the long journey through the countryside, having to worry about setting up camp or whether the rain will bog down the roads when they know there's a dragon to fight at the end.

This zoom-in/zoom-out trick isn't just DM magic; it's a pacing tool stolen straight from screenwriting. Treat your campaign like a fine-tuned, time-sensitive screenplay, where every scene reveals character, advances the plot, or cranks up the tension. If it doesn't do one of those things, it's just dead weight dragging your game down.

Zoom in for the stage directions - the rogue's shaky hand as they pick the lock, the paladin's glare as they confront their corrupted mentor, and zoom out for the time skips - "You spend a week on the road, the bard sings too much, and you eat jerky of questionable origin." Cut the dead weight, focus on what matters, and keep the session rolling at a pace that feels cinematic. Do this right, and your players won't just be along for the ride - they'll be gripping the edges of their seats, begging for the next scene to drop.

Now, some DMs like to keep things loose - despite spending an embarrassing amount of time plotting the whole campaign. Sometimes, in fact, you might *have* to keep things loose so you don't lose your mind when your players inevitably decide to do something unpredictable.

You already know your players *will* find ways to surprise you, break your carefully laid plans, and occasionally derail entire plot threads by trying to befriend the villain's pet dire ferret instead of fighting it. Don't panic. Improvise. Reincorporate elements they latched onto, shift your villain's scheme to accommodate their strange ally, or present consequences that feel earned. When you adapt gracefully, the players learn that their creativity genuinely affects the world - which is exactly what separates a great TTRPG campaign from a linear video game.

Let's say you planned a big showdown with a crime lord in the city's underbelly, but the party instead befriends his messenger and convinces them to spill the beans early. Now, the epic battle might not happen as planned. Instead, you can reveal that the crime lord, anticipating betrayal, left a trap behind - secret assassins who follow the party's every move. The final confrontation still occurs, but now it's laced with paranoia and tension built from the players' clever shortcut.

By executing on your careful design - keeping momentum, embracing player agency, pacing sessions well, delivering meaningful rewards, evolving your NPCs, and staying flexible - you'll transform your lovingly crafted blueprint into a living, breathing epic. Your players won't just be pieces on a board; they'll be heroes actively shaping the narrative, forging bonds with your NPCs, and conquering challenges on their own terms. And when the campaign finally concludes (preferably with a dragon — or at least a villain monologue so long it legally counts as a podcast), they'll look back fondly, remembering not just its grand design, but how thrilling it was to live and breathe its story.

Conclusion: From Plot Hooks to Glory

At the end of the day, building a longer campaign isn't just about piling content sky-high - it's about guiding your players through a journey that constantly evolves, surprises, and feels like it matters.

You're not only a Dungeon Master here; you're part game designer, part scriptwriter, part improv comedian, and part ringmaster of the world's most unpredictable circus. By layering hooks that linger, twisting the narrative when they least expect it, and cultivating NPCs who practically leap off the page (or screen) into your players' hearts, you keep that fire burning session after session.

There is a simple reason why you choose this guide - you *want* to be a great Dungeon Master. To get there, you've got to put in the work. The good news? The labor won't be backbreaking, but the work needs doing nonetheless.

Remember, great campaigns don't just happen. They're painstakingly constructed with forethought and flexibility. You're going to throw out some carefully laid plans when the party decides to team up with the goblins instead of fighting them or when that NPC you thought would be a one-and-done cameo becomes everyone's new best friend (or nemesis, depending on who rolled what). Don't fight that chaos - embrace it. Use it. Let your players help shape your masterpiece. They'll feel more invested, and you'll find fresh inspiration in their unexpected choices.

Long campaigns thrive on trust. Your players need to trust that you won't waste their time with meaningless slog, and you need to trust that they'll engage if you give them a reason to care. Show them that their actions have lasting consequences, that the big reveals are always earned, and that the journey is more than just a countdown to the final boss.

You've got this. I know sometimes being a Dungeon Master feels like juggling flaming swords while riding a unicycle on a tightrope made of your players' expectations,

113 | Creating Longer Campaigns

but guess what? You're already crushing it. You've built worlds, breathed life into characters, and turned random dice rolls into unforgettable moments of triumph, tragedy, and utter chaos.

And sure, maybe sometimes the plot veers off a cliff or your players latch onto the wrong NPC (looking at you, Gregor the Unintentionally Hot Goblin), but that's part of the magic. The messiness, the surprises, the sheer unpredictability - that's where the best stories are born. Keep going, keep weaving, and trust yourself. You're not just running a game; you're crafting a legend that'll echo around the table for years. And when in doubt, remember: a confident smirk and a well-timed "Are you sure?" can cover any plot hole.

You've got the tools now: the structure, the pacing, the tricks of the trade. So go forth, oh mighty DM, and craft a saga that your players will talk about for years - one that makes them laugh, gasp, cheer, and maybe even shed a tear or two. When they look back on your game, what you really want them to say is, "We lived through an epic, and it was glorious."

Chapter 3: Campaign Management

Congratulations, Dungeon Master. By now, you've survived the arduous journey of worldbuilding and creating a compelling campaign in your world. Your meticulously plotted story arcs have been gleefully dismantled, your maps have been shredded like incriminating evidence, and your grand narrative now looks like a detective's board with more red string than coherence.

But here's the thing: this chaos is only just beginning. Because once you've let players tear through your plans like sugar-fueled raccoons, it'll be time to manage the tangled mess they left in their wake. This, my friend, is where true Dungeon Mastery begins.

You're not just running a story, oh no. You're conducting a symphony of unpredictability. You are juggling plot threads, wrangling character arcs, and keeping track of every decision your players made while also trying to remember which NPC they accidentally promoted to "Most Important Person in the Universe" status. It's part storytelling, part logistics, and part "I'm just making this up as I go and hoping no one notices."

There's more to campaign management than just keeping track of plot twists and wayward NPCs, though. Your players - those wonderful, chaos-bringing gremlins - are an ever-evolving variable in this equation. They'll argue over loot, hog the spotlight, or decide mid-session that their bard needs a five-hour subplot about starting a lute-based pyramid scheme.

Keeping your world intact is one thing, but keeping your players engaged, cooperative, and invested is another beast entirely. You're not just managing the story - you're managing people. Their ideas, their personalities, and their weird vendettas against random goblins.

So, grab your notebook, your dice, and maybe a stress ball. It's time to step into the ring, tighten your Dungeon Master cape, and show this campaign - and your players - who's really in charge (it's still kind of them, but don't tell them that). Follow me, and I'll show you how to ensure their chaos becomes a story worth telling.

Adapting to Player Choices

Adapting to a player's choices is like being the tour guide in a fantasy theme park where your guests are a gaggle of sugar-fueled toddlers armed with boundless imagination and questionable impulse control. You've got your neatly plotted map, a bulletproof route, and a plan to hit all the highlight attractions: the Enchanted Forest, the Dragon's Lair, and maybe a side quest at the Whimsical Fountain of Narrative Significance.

It's all so orderly, so perfectly paced in your head. But just as you're heading for the Big Resolution Carousel, one of these sticky-fingered chaos agents spots a butterfly, shrieks "DRAGON!" at the top of their lungs, and bolts straight into the dense underbrush of the Unplanned Plotline.

Now, you have two choices: You could stick to your script and let them wander off to be devoured by the metaphoric wolves of disengagement, or you can roll up your sleeves, lace your boots a little tighter, and follow them into the narrative scrambler.

The real goal here is to have your players wondering if you're a world-class improviser or just a glorious masochist who secretly thrives on chaos. So off you go, frantically redrawing your map in real-time, scribbling out pathways like a caffeinated cartographer while the toddlers you are babysitting - err, I mean players - gleefully dismantle your meticulously planned story arc with the precision of a tiny, whimsical wrecking ball.

But here's the trick: when you embrace that unexpected detour, you're not just humoring random tangents - you're breathing life into the game. That butterfly-turned-dragon might lead to a hidden cave full of treasure, a new NPC who becomes central to the plot, or a side story that turns out more compelling than your original plan.

The world feels more alive because it *is* more alive, shaped by the chaotic energy of your players' whims and your ability to weave those whims into something meaningful. In the end, the "dragon" was never even on your radar, but now it's part of your world, a monument to spontaneity and shared storytelling.

So, when your players inevitably rip up your map and gallop into the narrative unknown, remember that you're not losing control - you're expanding the horizon. Your campaign isn't a railroad - it's a living, breathing landscape where the most memorable moments often come from the unplanned, the improvised, and the "Why not?" of it all.

Overall, it's all about *embracing* the chaos. I mean, sure, you could drag them back to your original plan, kicking and screaming. But where's the fun in that? Let them chase the butterflies, let them shout "DRAGON!" with reckless abandon, and you'll find that those wild, sugar-fueled tangents are what make your game unforgettable. And hey, who needs a plan when you've got a dragon? You just need to squint a little and pretend it was part of the plan all along.

Take this classic scenario. You've set up an epic quest where the party is supposed to explore the haunted forest and defeat the Shadow Wraith to save a kidnapped prince. You've got atmospheric descriptions ready: mist curling through ancient trees, the distant sound of owls, the scent of decaying leaves.

You're all but shaking with excitement at the thought of unleashing your spooky wraith voice. And then - because players are chaos incarnate - someone says, "Nah. Let's buy a boat and start a fishing business."

Now, you could stamp your foot and insist that they must go to the forest. But why not take the bait (pun fully intended) and let them become fantasy fishermen? Who says the Shadow Wraith can't haunt the high seas? Maybe the prince was kidnapped by pirates instead, or maybe the haunted forest is actually a cursed island that's only accessible by boat. Boom. The story is back on track, and your players are blissfully unaware that they've just led you on a wild goose chase.

Flexibility is the key to survival here. You need to be agile, adaptable, and ready to drop a quip when things get weird. You're not losing control; you're just redirecting the story. And honestly, the more your players feel like their choices matter, the more invested they'll be.

Sure, they're derailing your plans faster than a Pippin goes through a second breakfast, but that's part of the fun.

The best moments come from the unexpected. If they decide to fish instead of fight, well, make sure the fish bite back.

Speaking of the unexpected, let's talk about those moments when a random, throwaway NPC suddenly becomes the star of the show. You know the type. You create a blacksmith named Randy. He's got a mustache, a hammer, and exactly zero relevance to the plot. He exists solely to sell swords and send the party on their merry way. But then, one player decides that Randy is fascinating. They ask about his hobbies, his dreams, his tragic backstory. Suddenly, Randy is no longer a background character; he's the new party mascot. The next thing you know, they're inviting Randy on quests and suggesting that maybe he's the chosen one destined to defeat the Dark Lord.

Congratulations. Randy the blacksmith is now the most important person in your campaign.

When this happens - and it will happen - don't fight it. Roll with it. Give Randy a sprinkle of depth on the fly. Maybe his obsession with hammers comes from a traumatic childhood incident where a rogue anvil crushed his dad. Maybe he's an ex-paladin who hung up his holy sword because of a crisis of faith. You don't need a full biography, at least not right away. You can always develop him further between sessions. Just start with one or two juicy details that can turn Randy from a throwaway NPC to a compelling character.

And if your players decide that Randy is the chosen one, lean into the absurdity. Picture a sweaty blacksmith fumbling through heroics, completely out of his depth, while your rogue facepalms and your bard tries to hype him up with an off-key power ballad. It's comedy gold. And it all came from letting your players take the reins for a second.

Of course, sometimes your players' choices threaten to completely torpedo the campaign you so lovingly plotted out. You've got an intricate, multi-arc epic ready to unfold - full of twists, betrayals, and tear-jerking emotional payoffs. You can practically hear the dramatic orchestral score swelling in the background. And then your party decides that, instead of saving the kingdom from an ancient evil, they'd rather invest all their gold into starting a petting zoo for baby owlbears. At this point, you feel a vein pop in your forehead. *Why are they like this?* Are you being punished for wanting a cohesive narrative?

But here's the thing: player detours don't have to be campaign derailments. In fact, they can be the exact opposite. They can become the heart and soul of your campaign. Remember playing *Skyrim* and spending an ungodly number of hours helping some random peasant find their lost frying pan when you were supposed to be saving the world? Did it make sense? Not always. Did it make the world feel vibrant, lived-in, and immersive? Absolutely.

Your players' desire to run an absurd baby owlbear petting zoo can do the same thing. The trick is to find a way to tie their weird obsession back into the main plot. Maybe the owlbears are sacred creatures foretold in an ancient prophecy. Maybe the zoo attracts powerful nobles who have secret agendas. Maybe it's just a front for smuggling enchanted artifacts. Now, all of a sudden, their chaotic side hustle is narratively significant, and you look like a storytelling mastermind. (And don't *tell* them you're improvising at breakneck speed. They don't need to know; let them think this was your plan all along.)

Think of your campaign like a road trip. Sure, you've got a destination figured out, but the players are the ones picking the playlists, deciding where to stop for snacks, and occasionally veering off-course to see the Twenty Foot Beef Jerky at Buc-ee's (it's not one large piece of jerky, its many small pieces twenty feet long, they are liars and I'll never forgive them for the misleading billboards that derailed my trip to Florida).

As a DM, it is your job to make that jerky real. Maybe it's cursed, binding the fates of those who eat it. Maybe the flip side reveals a hidden map of the final dungeon. Maybe it's really, really tasty to give your party a brief moment of joy before they march off to inevitable doom. Or maybe it's enough that it even exists at all because *why* would you advertise twenty feet of jerky when it didn't really exist unless you were being *intentionally* misleading?! Anyway... whatever it is, embrace the detour. The best stories often come from the strangest stops along the way.

When your players veer left when you've clearly signposted a right turn, don't panic. Make left the most fascinating, plot-twisting, lore-packed place they could possibly wander into. It's not about forcing them back onto the road you mapped out. It's about showing them that every road has a story to tell.

Keep redrawing your mental map, keep turning their whims into opportunities, and remember that flexibility is your superpower. You're not a train conductor; you're a storyteller who thrives on chaos. When they chase a butterfly into the narrative wilderness, go with them and discover what's there. Who knows? That butterfly might be a shape-shifted fae queen or the herald of a world-ending event. Or maybe it's just a butterfly. That's fun, too.

Most importantly, keep having fun. If you're not enjoying the chaos, your players won't either. You're all co-pilots on this storytelling journey. Yes, you have the map and all-seeing vision, but they've got the wheel - and sometimes they'll take it off-road, through a swamp, and straight into the territory of the Goblin Mafia. Lean into it. Your players are telling *their* story; all you have to do is ensure it's one they'll remember. If they want to tell a tale about heroic blacksmiths, enchanted fishing rods, or, yes, a baby owlbear petting empire, who are you to stand in the way of greatness?

Ultimately, campaigns thrive when players' choices matter. Even if their choices seem ludicrous, finding ways to validate them strengthens their investment. When they see that their petting zoo shenanigans ripple out into the world, they know they're not just passengers - they're world-shapers. That's the magic of tabletop RPGs: the shared, chaotic, unpredictable authorship. When their silly decisions become legendary moments, they'll remember *that* more than any pre-planned plot twist you had up your sleeve.

So, let them chase their ridiculous dreams. Let them build petting zoos, fish for mythical trout, or detour into a five-hour debate about medieval plumbing systems. Because the moment you embrace their chaos and weave it back into your narrative, you're not losing control - you're giving the story a life of its own. And isn't that what makes it all worth it?

Adapting to player choices means you're already careening headfirst through a narrative obstacle course with a smile and a map that's rapidly becoming obsolete. The moment your players turn Randy the Blacksmith into the Chosen One, you're in deep improvisational waters.

While it's fun to chase those butterflies into chaos, that chaos has a nasty habit of building up, intertwining, and threatening to turn your beautifully planned campaign into a tangled mess of forgotten NPCs and unresolved side plots. This is where the real challenge begins: keeping track of it all. Because once you've embraced the chaos, you'll need a way to manage the ever-evolving complexity of the world you've just unleashed.

When your world is a tangled web of NPCs, forgotten plot hooks, and side quests gone rogue, it's easy to feel like you're one misstep away from total chaos. But here's the twist: that chaos is driven by your players. Their decisions, debates, and dynamics are the fuel that keeps your campaign burning bright - or sometimes burning down.

The next challenge isn't just managing the world; it's managing the people sitting around the table, making sure everyone's voice gets heard, conflicts get resolved, and nobody ends up feeling like a background character in someone else's epic. Because a great campaign isn't just a well-run world; it's a well-run group.

Managing the Ever-Evolving Complexity of the World and the Campaign

Managing campaign complexity is like juggling flaming swords while riding a unicycle on a tightrope over a pit of lava.

This is where you become part ringmaster, part detective, and part caffeine-fueled insomniac desperately trying to remember if the NPC from two sessions ago was supposed to be a villain, a hero, or just a guy who sold cheese. But fear not! I'm here to walk you through the fire and the cheese with some tried-and-true advice on keeping your campaign organized and coherent, even when the plot is spinning out like a Michael Bay movie.

First, let's talk about keeping notes. Yes, notes. You know, those scribbly little things you were forced to take in school but never actually read. Well, guess what? Now they're your lifeline.

If you aren't keeping track of what happens each session, your campaign is basically a ship without a compass, floating aimlessly toward the Island of Plot Holes. And when you inevitably crash there, your players will look at you with those innocent eyes and ask, "Wait, wasn't the blacksmith named Randy? " And you'll break into a cold sweat because you could've sworn he was Roger.

Or was it Richard? Yeah, you've got to do something about that. Even if it looks overwhelming, just remember that you can always start with something simple. After each session, take 10-15 minutes to jot down a quick recap: who the players met, what decisions they made, and what chaos they unleashed upon your carefully planned world.

Keep it short and punchy. Something like, "Players turned an innocent cabbage merchant into a cult leader. City now in chaos. Randy the Blacksmith is still inexplicably alive." Don't overthink it.

The point is to have a cheat sheet for the next session, so you're not left floundering when someone asks, "So what happened last time? " And for the love of all that is nerdy, write down your NPCs' names. I don't care if they're minor background characters like "Bart the Bartender" or "Steve the Street Urchin." The moment you name them, commit their names to paper (or word doc.)

Because if you don't, your players will. And suddenly, Steve Urchin has an entire subplot involving a lost inheritance and a quest for vengeance against the corrupt Duke of Butzland, and you'll have no idea where it came from.

Let's talk about organizing your notes. Some DMs love the tactile joy of a physical notebook. And hey, if you've got a leather-bound tome with ominous runes on the cover, more power to ya. Nothing says "master planner," like dramatically flipping open a grimoire of session notes.

But even if your notebook is just a battered spiral with coffee stains and an ominous smudge that you hope is pizza sauce, the key is consistency. Use sticky notes, tabs, or just scrawl big, obvious headers: "Session Recaps," "NPCs," "Plot Hooks," "Random Stuff My Players Did That I Need to Fix Later."

127 | *Campaign Management*

If you're more of a digital note-taker, keep it simple. MS Word, Google Docs, or Excel will do just fine. Create a document for each campaign and organize it with clear sections. You can have one for session summaries, one for NPCs, one for plot arcs, and a special section titled "Player Shenanigans" for those times when they decide to kidnap a talking chicken and appoint it mayor. Pro tip: use bold, underlines, and color-coding to make important stuff stand out. Future You will thank you. You don't want to have to scroll through five minutes of the wall of text to find that one note about how Randy the Blacksmith was secretly an ex-paladin.

Now, let's get into the ever-growing plot web. You know what I mean: your players are merrily pulling on story threads, and you now have a tangled mess of subplots, side quests, and half-baked ideas that somehow all connect to each other. It's like you're building the conspiracy wall from *It's Always Sunny in Philadelphia*, complete with frenzied glances and frantic gestures toward bits of string and thumbtacks.

A helpful hint here is to actually map it out. Get a sheet of paper, or launch a simple drawing tool, and begin to visualize the linkages between these plot points. Draw circles for the major NPCs, quests, and locations, and then link them with lines.

For example, "Shadow Wraith" connects to "Kidnapped Prince," which connects to "Haunted Forest" which connects to "Players Refused to Enter Forest and Bought a Boat Instead." Now you have a visual representation of how everything links together - or doesn't.

If it looks like the scribblings of a madman, you're on the right track. And when the web starts getting too tangled, don't be afraid to prune the plot tree. Not every thread needs to lead somewhere. Sometimes, the players' obsession with the cabbage merchant doesn't need a payoff. It's okay to let some things fade into the background.

Focus on the arcs that matter most to your story and your players' characters. Otherwise, you'll end up drowning in details and driving yourself bonkers trying to make everything fit.

Next up... session prep. You don't need to prep everything - you just need to prep enough. It's a delicate balance; you'll learn through experience, but start by focusing on the key beats for the next session: where are the players likely to go, who they are likely to meet, and what's the next big twist or reveal?

Jot down the essentials, but leave room for improvisation. If... *When* your players go off-script, you don't want to be so locked into your plan that you can't pivot. And let's not forget the most important tool for managing complexity: your players themselves. That's right, offload some of the mental burden onto them. Encourage your players to take notes, keep track of NPC names, and remind you of the bonkers stuff they did.

If someone volunteers to maintain an exhaustive campaign journal, be sure to play it cool. Grant them inspiration points, praise them to the heavens, bow at their feet, buy them dinner, hell, even do their laundry. They are your lifeline, your memory bank, and your insurance against the inevitable brain farts.

Campaign complexity becomes less about keeping everything tied up with a bow and more about maintaining what's left of your sanity. Whether it's in a dust-covered notebook or an artfully color-coded spreadsheet, the ultimate point is just to keep the story moving, the players active, and those flaming swords from becoming rubber chickens. And when all else fails, write something down, tie it up with some string, and hope nobody figures out that you really had nothing planned all along.

Managing Player Dynamics

Managing player dynamics is like running a reality TV show where everyone is armed with swords, magic spells, and far too much knowledge about obscure fantasy lore. Your job as the Dungeon Master is to keep the peace, maintain the drama, and, if necessary, flip the metaphorical table and exclaim, "Well, Well, Well... How the turntables..."

Whether you've got a table full of extroverts battling for the spotlight, a shy group of wallflowers who'd rather chew on their dice than role-play, or a mix of both, you're going to need strategies. And patience. And maybe a drink.

Let's start with large parties. You know the kind: six or more players all excitedly shouting ideas at once. It's like being a kindergarten teacher on Free Balloon Day, except the kids have magic, and one of them is threatening to Eldritch Blast the mayor. The challenge here is making sure everyone gets their moment. You don't want your game to become the "Look At My Awesome Character" show featuring your most vocal player while the others quietly drift into a fugue state.

The trick is to manage the spotlight like a DJ at a club. Keep the beats flowing, but make sure each player gets their turn on the dance floor. When someone's hogging the scene, gently redirect. "Alright, Leeroy Jenkins, let's hold off on threatening the mayor for a second. What's Ethel the Rogue up to?"

If you sense a quieter player is getting overshadowed, set them up for a moment of glory. Maybe a secret passage only they notice, or a riddle only they can solve because of their ability to speak draconic.

And when all else fails, break the party up. I am against giving that advice to beginner DMs, but since *you* are not a beginner, listen closely because split-screen storytelling is a true and powerful savior.

While splitting a party isn't easy and is frankly kind of terrifying to think about, it isn't the end of the world. There are perfectly reasonable ways to do it. Maybe your rogue went off to seduce information out of a smarmy noble while the barbarian decided to test the structural integrity of a local tavern with their fists. Now you're juggling two simultaneous threads, and instead of a tidy, linear narrative, you've got branching chaos on your hands. But here's the thing: splitting the party, when done right, is a storytelling superpower.

Imagine each group's perspective as scenes in a high-octane heist film. One half is sneaking through laser-guarded hallways, sweat dripping as they inch towards the vault, while the other half distracts the clueless guards with a perfectly timed argument over whose turn it is to buy lunch. The trick is to keep both sides feeling connected and relevant while making each group feel like the heroes of their own subplot. Done well, split-screen sessions create tension, excitement, and those delicious "oh no, what are they doing?" moments that'll have your players on the edge of their seats.

Balance is the key to avoiding the dreaded player boredom spiral. You don't want one group to feel like they're starring in a blockbuster while the other is stuck watching paint dry. When you switch between the groups, try to end each scene on a cliffhanger or a moment of suspense - something that makes them desperate to know what happens next.

Time management is your secret weapon here. Don't spend an hour with one group while the other stares into the existential void of idle dice. Think of it like flipping channels during a tense sports game - keep the pace brisk, and give each group five to ten minutes of focus before switching back. This rhythm keeps everyone engaged and prevents players from mentally wandering off to ponder snack logistics.

Speaking of engagement, keep everyone involved, even when they're "off-screen." Encourage players to pay attention to each other's scenes. Drop hints, clues, or shared stakes that'll make both sides feel invested in the outcome. If the rogue's stealth mission is secretly setting up the barbarian's brawl, let that connection shine through. Nothing feels cooler than realizing both sides of the party are unknowingly working towards the same explosive conclusion.

Now, for the grand finale: bring it all crashing back together in a glorious mess of plot threads. Maybe the rogue's stealth mission goes sideways and spills into the tavern while the barbarian is mid-bar fight. Suddenly, the two narratives collide in a chaotic free-for-all of accusations, flying chairs, and improvised teamwork. It's moments like these where split-screen storytelling feels less like juggling and more like orchestrating a masterful double-cross in a spy movie.

The real beauty of splitting the party is that it lets your players shine individually before weaving them back together for a shared triumph (or shared catastrophe, depending on their decisions). Either way, it'll be memorable, chaotic, and the kind of moment they'll talk about long after the dice stop rolling. Let's just hope the chaos stays in game.

Let's face it, players can argue about anything. So let's talk about resolving conflicts at the table. Whether it's rules, loot, or if they should spare or stab the obviously evil NPC who just offered them tea. Players are bound to have some disagreements. I once had a party spend 45 minutes debating whether a goblin deserved mercy after stealing a single silver piece. It was like *Judge Judy: Fantasy Edition*. One of my players even drew up a flowchart on why Goopy the Goblin should perish. These moments can be hilarious, but they can also get heated, especially if someone's feeling personally slighted.

When tempers flare, your job is to step in and play the role of mediator. Channel your inner Obi-Wan Kenobi: calm, wise, and just a little bit disappointed in everyone's life choices. Remind your players that, ultimately, you're all here to have fun. If the argument is about rules, pause, look it up (or make a ruling on the fly), and move on. No one wants a three-hour debate over whether someone can or cannot cast Fireball underwater (they probably can, just have the druid warn the fish first).

But what if it's not about rules? What if it's about feelings? Well, that's where things get trickier. Sometimes, players' *characters* clash because the players *themselves* are clashing. Maybe Person A is annoyed that Person B always gets the last hit on the big bad. Maybe Person C thinks Person D's rogue is stealing all the glory (and the gold).

In these cases, it might be best to just take a break. Step away from the table, have a quick chat with the players involved, and remind them that in-game drama shouldn't bleed into real-life resentment. And if it does? Well, that's what side quests are for. Split the party for a few sessions and let things cool off. Maybe Person A's barbarian goes on a solo spirit quest while Person B's wizard solves a magical mystery. Everyone wins - including you because it's easier to schedule solo quest sessions with a single player or small group anyway.

Speaking of which, let's shift gears to smaller parties. We're talking two or three players, maybe even one, either because you are running a campaign with a smaller party or you split the huge party up and scheduled their sessions separately for a few weeks. This is where things get intimate.

135 | Campaign Management

And by intimate, I mean you have to work twice as hard because there's nowhere to hide. If one player decides to zone out, your entire session suddenly becomes a one-on-one therapy session between you and Mark's depressed bard, who just wants to play sad lute music in peace.

Running a small party means tailoring the story to the players' strengths and giving them room to shine. With fewer characters, each player's backstory and choices carry more weight. Don't be afraid to lean into it. If you've got a solo player, give them a rich, personal narrative full of moral dilemmas, deep character development, and way too many NPCs who know their name.

Combat can get tricky, though. Fewer players mean fewer chances to cover all the bases. No healer? No tank? No problem! Adjust the encounters to fit their skill sets, or throw in an NPC sidekick to balance things out. Just make sure the sidekick doesn't steal the show. No one wants to be upstaged by NPC Kevin, no matter how cool his backstory about avenging his pet beaver might be.

Remember that pacing is everything in small parties. There's less chatter and less chaos, so things move faster. Be ready to improvise if they blaze through your planned encounters in 20 minutes (or, more likely, walk right past them). Throw in some character-driven side plots. Maybe a mysterious letter arrives. Maybe an old enemy resurfaces. Or maybe - just maybe - Kevin's pet beaver's ghost returns for revenge. (I don't know why I'm stuck on the beaver thing. I think I'm still mad about Buc-ee's jerky. Just roll with it.)

While I did present the campaigns as sorted by party size as large and small, there is a third kind - solo campaigns. Sometimes, it's just hard to find enough people to play with, and you might resort to playing with just one other person, or maybe you are trying your hand at splitting the party so each player can have their own session one week. Well, good news everyone, single-player campaigns are not only possible but can also be enjoyable, *if* you do a good job.

Running a single-person campaign is like being the showrunner for a one-hero epic. The spotlight is always on them, so make sure the story is all about their character's goals, flaws, and backstory. They're the Frodo, the Geralt, the John McClane of this journey - everything should feel personal and tailored to their arc.

Since they're solo, scale your challenges wisely. Group-level fights? That's a fast track to a funeral. Use fewer enemies, give them weaknesses, or make encounters solvable with brains instead of brawn. And don't be afraid to toss in an NPC sidekick for a little backup - someone who can heal, fight, or just yell, "Look out!" at the right time.

When they fail a roll, fail forward. Don't halt the action; complicate it. The trap they missed? Maybe it grazes them instead of impaling them. The guard they tried to bribe?

He'll help, but he wants a favor later. Just remember to keep the tension without crushing their spirit.

Solo heroes burn through resources fast, so sprinkle in rest opportunities and loot. Healing potions, kind innkeepers, enchanted wells - give them a chance to recover, or you'll end up with a very dead protagonist.

Lastly, pace it out. Solo play moves fast, so break up the action with downtime, NPC chats, or dramatic brooding sessions by the fire. If all else fails, let an NPC swoop in for a breather, deus ex machina style. Even the Lone Hero deserves a little help sometimes.

When done right, solo campaigns can be one of the most fulfilling ways to play an RPG. They either allow you to take a specific player through a campaign you've crafted just for them or can be a way for a large party to split off for a bit and have tons to talk about when they finally meet up again. That's a little DM secret for you; they can't metagame if they weren't there for the session.

Finally, let's talk about the wild card in every group: player engagement. One week, everyone's hyped, rolling natural 20s like they're going out of style. The next week, half the table looks like they've been hit with a Sleep spell. Maybe it's life stuff. Maybe it's burnout. Maybe it's because you didn't bring snacks. (Always bring snacks.)

To keep everyone engaged, mix things up. Throw in different types of challenges. If they're tired of combat, give them a juicy mystery to solve or a moral dilemma to wrestle with. If they've been talking their way out of everything, drop a giant unreasonably angry owlbear in their path and watch them panic. Change the pace, change the stakes, and above all, make sure their characters' choices matter. When players see their actions shaping the world, they stay hooked.

In the end, if engagement still dips, talk to your players. Maybe they want more role-play. Maybe they want less. Maybe they just want a break. That's okay. Sometimes, the best way to manage player dynamics is to acknowledge that we're all just a bunch of nerds trying to have fun, or sometimes, the only thing your campaign is missing is the banning of cell phones at the table. So take a breath, pass the snacks, put away the smartphones, and remember: when in doubt, always blame the jerky.

Conclusion: The Aftermath of Mayhem

Congratulations, Dungeon Master - you've wrestled chaos, untangled spaghetti plots, and kept your players from turning the table into a scene from *Survivor*. We tackled adapting to player choices (say yes to their weird ideas), managing campaign complexity (take notes or perish), and wrangling player dynamics (spotlight control, conflict resolution, and snacks - always snacks).

Remember: you're not here to control the story; you're here to shape it. Be part improv comedian and part detective, and when things go sideways, just smile knowingly like you totally saw it coming. The best campaigns thrive on unexpected twists, half-baked plans, and players who decide the random cabbage merchant deserves his own heroic arc.

So take a breath, embrace the chaos, and when all else fails - fake it 'til you make it. You've totally got this. And if you don't? Don't worry; they'll never know the difference.

Chapter 4:
Crafting a Great Session

You've built your world; you have a campaign that's longer than a wizard's beard and more tangled than... a wizard's beard. Your players have an intense hankering to dive into the next session like hungry goblins at a free buffet. Now, all that's left is to create one of those sessions that is so good and memorable that your players will be talking about it for years.

No pressure.

A great session isn't just about what happens in the game - it's about how it feels to be at the table. It's about making those few hours of gameplay feel like stepping into another world. You're the DM, the master of ceremonies, the director of chaos, and the person responsible for turning random dice rolls and half-baked ideas into a story that sings.

The stuff I will recommend here isn't all that cheap, but don't worry about it. Fancy stuff isn't the key to a great session - it's the effort you put into making it great. Relying on DIY principles can make your players truly appreciate the work you put into the table - both in terms of the snacks *and* the session you're going to run for them. But this is the *advanced* guide, after all, so I'll be sure to give you both big and small-budget options to choose from.

This chapter is your guide to making every session epic. We'll talk about setting the mood, balancing preparation and improvisation, keeping combat snappy and thrilling, and throwing in enough twists and quirks to keep your players on the edge of their seats. Grab your dice, your notes, your snacks, and the slightly worse snacks you leave out for your players, and let's craft your own legendary session.

Creating an Atmosphere: Setting the Scene

Imagine you're setting the stage for your session. Your players walk in, ready to roll some dice and wreck your plans. Only, instead of seeing a plain table and hearing the clatter of dice, they step into a dimly lit room reverberating with the low hum of fantasy music, flickering candlelight, and the faint scent of freshly baked bread (or maybe burnt pizza rolls - we've all been there).

As if they stepped through a magical portal, they are in your world. Atmosphere is your secret weapon to make a game night not just ordinary but immersive. Here's how to set the stage like a pro.

Music: The Soundtrack of Epic Adventures

Nothing sets the mood for a session quite like the right music. You don't need a live orchestra in your living room - unless you've got one on standby, in which case, please invite me over; I play a mean cello - but a well-chosen playlist can turn your average game night into an epic saga faster than you can say, "roll for initiative."

Picture this: your players settle in, the lights are low, and soft, eerie strains of music drift through the room. In a heartbeat, they're no longer just sitting at your table walled in by empty soda cans - they're in your misty forest, dank dungeon, or rowdy tavern where the barmaid's a little too friendly.

When the swords start clanging in a life-or-death clash, and the dice start to fly, you want battle music that hits harder than a Barbarian mid-rage. It's time for something intense, something that makes your players feel like they're in a fight for their lives. Or, at least, for their loot.

Whether it's soaring orchestral scores, pounding drums, or something that sounds like it's coming from a blacksmith's personal hype playlist, the goal is adrenaline.

If their hearts aren't racing and they're not gripping their dice like their lives depend on it, you're not doing it right.

My favorite trick to pull off is to create an NPC entrance, especially for villains, and give them their own theme music, Darth Vader style. When that low, menacing, rhythmic melody creeps in, and you see your players exchanging nervous looks... That's when you'll *know* you have created a great atmosphere.

If you can find the right musical motif, you can use it to trigger the perfect emotional response in your players. Dread when a new enemy emerges, excitement when they finally crack that puzzle, or pure, simmering spite when their nemesis outsmarts them yet again. Just like Vader can have his own custom music, your players can have their own heroic theme. Nothing makes a player's head swell with pride quite like their own personal soundtrack kicking in when they finally land a blow on the Big Bad.

But here's the thing: sometimes, the best soundtrack is nothing at all. When the tension peaks, silence can do the job better than any melody. Let the room fall quiet, let the weight of the moment settle, and watch your players start sweating under the pressure. No music, just the sound of dice knocking together while someone nervously clears their throat - it's the kind of vibe that makes even the bravest adventurer second-guess their choices.

Naturally, silence only works when the other scenes have had an epic soundtrack. If you spent the entire session in silence, then there is nothing to contrast off of. The key is to find the balance between ambient noise, music, and intentional silence.

When it comes to balancing which music to use to set the stage, you want to be ready for anything. Exploration, combat, mysteries, downtime - have something queued up for all of it. With a quick click or tap, you can shift the entire vibe of the session.

Believe it or not, there are apps on your phone that will do it all for you. My favorite is called Pocket Bard. It's a simple program you can use to insert the right ambient noise, background music, or even fully vocalized song for any occasion. Whether it's windswept mountain trails or stormy seas, they have options to bring any setting you have to life. The best thing about it is that you can use one-off sound effects when you need to emphasize the gravity of a moment. I discovered Pocket Bard at a convention a few years ago. I downloaded their app because they were amazing people, and wow - best decision ever. I've been using it ever since, and it just keeps getting better.

Apps like this save you the legwork, but you can always do things the old-fashioned way and cobble together a Spotify playlist and dig through online soundboards. Just brace yourself for a marathon of brain-melting meme noises before you unearth that perfect thunderclap.

Whether it's a subtle backdrop, an intense battle score, or that sweat-inducing silence, music is your co-DM. Use it wisely, switch it boldly, and when all else fails, just pick something that feels epic and pretend it was part of the plan all along. And if you need to create an epic moment, what's better than flicking the light switch off and on? Well, actually... a lot.

Lighting: Because Fluorescent Bulbs Aren't Very Epic

Picture your players descending into an ancient crypt, torches in hand, ready to face whatever horrors await, but instead of a shadowy, ominous atmosphere, you've got fluorescent lights buzzing overhead like a discount dentist's office. Nothing says "adventure" quite like the feeling you might be asked to rinse and spit at any moment. If you want to avoid that vibe-killing scenario, you need to master the art of lighting.

First, let's talk candles. Real, honest-to-goodness candles are perfect for that warm, flickering glow that makes everyone feel like they've time-traveled to a medieval inn. The flame dances, shadows twist, and suddenly your table is less "suburban living room" and more "tavern where someone's about to get punched."

Of course, there's always the risk of your players accidentally summoning the fire department because someone leaned too close to the flame while over-dramatically mimicking their character's death. If fire hazards and charred character sheets aren't your idea of a good time, LED candles are your salvation. You buy them once, they flicker, they glow, and they don't turn your game into an impromptu lesson in fire safety.

If you want maximum control, dimmable lights are your new best friend. Regular old bulbs are fine for when everyone's in a cheerful village square, but the moment they step into a cursed battlefield or an underwater cave, you'll want to tweak the vibe. Drop the lights low and watch everyone hunch forward, suddenly aware of how creepy things just got.

Obviously, getting some of this extra stuff can be expensive and time-consuming, but don't be alarmed; there are far cheaper alternatives. There are plenty of DIY lighting possibilities from intricately crafted disco balls to a flashlight pointed at your chin. Hell, if you have a TV or a laptop you can use, there are a bunch of atmospheric videos on YouTube that you can use to your advantage. Just dim the lights and let the video of a crackling fire illuminate your room (you know the one). Just be careful which videos you choose, or a poorly timed *Raid Shadow Legends* ad may ruin your immersion.

Smart lights let you take it even further: crimson glows for battles drenched in blood and fire, cold blue for submerged ruins where the air feels thick and oppressive, or a sickly green for enchanted forests where everything looks like it might be watching. With just a click, your living room transforms into a place of life-or-death situations.

And for the truly brave (or just those who enjoy making their players suffer), nothing beats the power of darkness. Horror sessions, stealth missions, or any scenario where the unknown lurks just out of sight - these moments scream for pitch black.

Obviously, don't turn the lights completely off. Hand your players flashlights or lanterns and let them explore with only the beams of light they control. They'll be squinting into the shadows, jumping at every flicker, and suddenly realizing that the dungeon feels a lot less fun when they can only see what their "torch" illuminates. It's all fun and games until someone says, "My character has Darkvision," or the flashlight battery dies.

I'll never forget the night I had my players descend into an ancient, cursed ruin. The setup was perfect: crumbling archways, the air thick with dread, as I spun a yarn about torchlight flickering in the oppressive darkness. Except there wasn't any actual darkness - my living room lights were still blazing like I was lighting up a sports event.

Nothing says "impending doom" like harsh fluorescents and a bag of Cool Ranch Doritos gleaming on the table.

Mid-description, without breaking stride, I leaned back and killed the lights. Snap. Instant gloom. Shadows swallowed the table. The fighter tensed up, the bard stopped chewing mid-crunch, and everyone's eyes darted around like they half-expected something to crawl out from under the couch. That's when I knew it was working.

My secret? Don't announce it. No dramatic, "Hold on, let me hit the lights." Just do it. Lighting changes should land with the subtlety of a rogue's dagger - sudden, smooth, and slightly unsettling. If you fumble around, muttering about light switches and ambiance settings, the immersion shatters faster than a wizard's concentration in a bar fight.

To seal the vibe, I tossed a Bluetooth speaker under the table and hit play on a track of low, echoing drips and an unsettling hum. That's when the druid leaned in, eyes narrowing. "Do you hear that?" she whispered, like the sound wasn't coming from my $20 speaker. Perfect.

Of course, timing is everything. Once, in a similar setup, I aimed for darkness and accidentally triggered my smart bulb's "Party Mode." Nothing says "ancient horror" like an eldritch beast emerging under pulsing rainbow strobes. Try recovering the tension when your players are headbanging instead of trembling. The best recovery I could think of was to turn him into a disco-loving queen, but the damage was already done.

But when it lands, it lands. The combination of sudden darkness and ambient dread had my players clutching their dice, hearts pounding, fully convinced they were moments away from becoming part of the ruin's tragic history. Lighting and music aren't just tools; they're stealthy co-conspirators in your tale of terror. Use them right, and you'll drag your players into the shadows, where they'll squint, sweat, and wonder why they ever thought a homebrew dungeon would be fun.

So ditch the dentist's office vibes and embrace lighting that sets the stage for adventure, dread, or whatever brand of chaos you've cooked up for the night. Your players might not remember the exact plot twist you threw at them, but they'll never forget the eerie glow of candlelight or the oppressive darkness that made them genuinely question their life choices. And that's a win in any DM's book.

Props: Immersion You Can Touch

Props aren't just for theater kids or that one friend who insists on cosplaying at every opportunity (of course, that friend is me; who's asking?) The right prop, introduced at the right moment, can transport your players into your fantasy realm like a Portkey. They'll go from "Oh cool, a clue" to "I am holding *evidence* in my hands" faster than a rogue reaching for a loosely dangled coin purse.

The most obvious things are letters and scrolls. You could just describe an NPC's message in your best cryptic voice, but why *tell* when you can *show*? Hand your players a letter written in looping, sinister handwriting on parchment that looks like it survived a fire (or a coffee spill - no judgment).

Bonus points if you seal it with a wax stamp or spritz it with an unsettlingly mysterious scent. There's something about physically unfolding a letter that makes it feel less like a plot point and more like a personal summons to adventure (or doom, depending on how mean you're feeling).

And nothing whispers *"Get ready to quest"* like a weathered map or a cryptic clue. If you slap down a treasure map that looks like it's been crumpled, torn, and dragged through three tavern brawls, your players' eyes will light up like goblins spotting unguarded loot. Maybe the ink's smeared, or there's a cryptic X marking a spot that absolutely, positively promises death or riches - possibly both.

Tossing these kinds of props on the table turns a simple clue into something that demands to be solved. Now your players are leaning in, squinting at your coffee-stained artistry, trying to piece together a mystery like caffeine-fueled detectives.

Then again, there are also physical items. Coins that clink when they hit the table, keys that look like they unlock nightmares, clear potions with strong smells that make you sing *Purple Rain* in the worst falsetto known to man.

I once gave one of my players a rubber duck to represent an idol they looted from a dungeon. Why? Because I had it handy and thought it could represent loot well enough. "It's just a bath toy," I thought, tossing it to the bard. He cradled it reverently and declared, "This is Quackers, the Oracle of Suds." I laughed, the bard laughed, the whole party laughed.

But soon, they were consulting the duck for every major decision. Battle strategies? Quackers. Dungeon paths? Quackers. I threw in a riddle that should've taken hours. Instead, the bard shook the duck and said, "Quackers says left." They were right. I still don't know how. By the end of the campaign, this yellow oracle had a backstory, a shrine, and a level of respect I still strive to achieve.

You can easily incorporate physical items into your session. Say your rogue swipes a cursed dagger, and instead of just nodding, you actually hand them a (plastic) dagger. The look on their face? Pure gold. It's a mix of triumph, awe, and just a touch of *"Oh no, what have I done?"* That's the moment they stop thinking of their character as pixels or paper and start thinking of them as someone who's *actually* holding something dangerous.

But here's the trick - don't go full Broadway production. A handful of well-placed props is immersive; an entire replica dungeon set complete with dry ice and animatronics is *distracting*.

You want your players to feel like they've dipped a toe into your world, not that they've wandered into a Renaissance Faire with an identity crisis. If you find them spending more time admiring your origami treasure chests than actually opening them, you've probably gone too far.

So, embrace the power of props, but keep it simple. A letter here, a map there, maybe a shiny coin or a dusty tome. They'll feel the world closing in around them, and you'll feel like the puppet master you were born to be. Plus, the look on their faces when they hold that dagger? Worth every single second you spent scouring craft stores and wondering if hot glue burns count as battle scars.

Food: Because Snacks Are Sacred

Food might not seem like a tool for immersion, but trust me - it's a secret weapon disguised as a snack tray. The right snacks can turn a regular game night into a full-on sensory experience and keep your players from devolving into hangry goblins. Let's be honest here - a party with grumbling stomachs is a party that's not paying attention to your carefully crafted plot twist. Nothing shatters immersion faster than someone interrupting your villain's monologue with, "So, uh, do we have chips?"

If your party is feasting in a royal hall, don't just throw out a bag of pretzels and call it a day. Go for bread, cheese, and grapes - simple, elegant, and just pretentious enough to make everyone feel like minor nobility. Of course, if you can't afford an expensive charcuterie board, just cut up some string cheese. If you did everything right, your players will still feel like they're attending a prestigious gala.

When they're trudging through a dwarven mine, break out some beef jerky and root beer. It's rugged, it's hearty, and it's got just the right amount of chew to make everyone feel like they're gnawing through layers of rock.

And if they're wandering through a fey forest filled with whimsical danger, toss in some colorful candies and fresh fruit. Nothing says "enchanted woodland" like a handful of gummy worms and a few apple slices.

But snacks aren't just fuel - they're rewards, too. When someone rolls a natural 20, why not celebrate with a "crit cookie"? It's a little taste of victory and sugar-fueled dopamine. On the flip side, when they roll a natural 1, pass them a "failure chip." It should be stale, sad, and full of regret. Something that tastes like poor life choices and crushed dreams. It's a gentle reminder that sometimes fate is cruel and also that you probably should have checked the expiration date.

Hydration is just as important as snacks, because epic quests are thirsty work. Keep drinks handy - mead for the brave souls who like to live in character, sparkling cider for the sober-minded (or underage), and water because, well, at least one of us has to stay *actually* hydrated. And let's not forget "potions" - also known as fruit juice in a bottle that looks vaguely mystical. Nothing makes a player feel like a heroic adventurer more than chugging a "health potion" and pretending it's anything other than apple juice.

One critical piece of advice, though: avoid messy foods. I cannot emphasize this enough. No one wants to see nacho cheese smeared across their painstakingly drawn map or, worse, their character sheet. Imagine trying to justify how the rogue's dexterity score has become nothing more than an unreadable, greasy smear. It's a tragic tale of hubris and poor snack choices.

So, embrace the power of snacks. The right food keeps your players immersed, your table happy, and your story flowing. Plus, when the inevitable chaos hits and your entire party wipes, at least you'll have some cookies to soften the blow.

Visual Aids: Seeing Is Believing

When words fail, visuals swagger in like a bard who knows they've got the highest charisma at the table. You can spend five minutes describing the haunted forest, weaving a verbal tapestry about gnarled trees, ominous shadows, and the sense that something definitely wants to eat the party - or you can slap down an image of a creepy, mist-filled forest and let your players' brains fill in the dread on their own. Sometimes, a single picture can do the narrative heavy lifting faster and better than your most elaborate description.

Having a visual reference for important locations, NPCs, or those monsters that are too horrifying to properly put into words without resorting to tortured metaphors can save you from fumbling over your own descriptions like a barbarian who crit-failed an Intelligence saving throw.

One look at a picture of a storm-battered castle or a grizzled innkeeper with shifty eyes, and suddenly, everyone's on the same page. It's a quick, silent way of saying, "Yep, this is what you're up against," and watching that moment of clarity click into place. No more fumbling through awkward descriptions of an ogre whose face resembles a frying pan mishap - just show the image, and boom, they get it.

If you're really feeling ambitious, you can build entire collections of visuals to set the vibe for your campaign.

Think of it like making a mood board, except instead of planning a wedding or redesigning a living room, you're curating images of cursed forests, eldritch horrors, and taverns that smell like despair and bad decisions. Sharing these boards with your players before the session lets them marinate in the setting and show up already primed for adventure. It's a sneaky and often highly successful way to get them caring about your worldbuilding, and who doesn't love a little narrative subterfuge?

Whether you're a digital art wizard or someone who relies on the magical powers of "Google Image Search: Fantasy Edition," visuals are your trusty sidekick. They add texture, clarity, and sometimes pure, unfiltered terror to your game. And isn't that what we're all here for?

Using digital aids to get your point across naturally extends to using screens to assist you - whether it's a laptop, tablet, TV screen, or just your phone. You can use those additional screens to enhance the overall atmosphere. If you have a TV in the background that you can use to play a looping video of a snowstorm, you'll have a dose of immersion a single picture can't do. If a picture is worth 1000 words, imagine how many words you can milk out of that video.

Visual aids aren't strictly tied to 2D images, either. Nothing says "this fight matters," like slamming a mini of a towering dragon onto the table and watching your players' eyes widen in collective panic.

Equipment: Bringing the World to Life

The lights are dim, shadows dance on the walls, and the music hums with the promise of adventure. Snacks are disappearing faster than mead after a hard-won battle. The stage is set, and the tension is so taught that it can be plucked like a string. Now's the time to unleash the tools that will make your world explode into vivid reality. This is where "Hey, let's pretend" explodes into "Oh gods, this is getting real." Where your table becomes a realm of sight, sound, touch, and heart-pounding reality. All of a sudden, no one's just playing a game anymore; it's become something far more significant.

Minis, maps, and terrain aren't just for show; they're the spark that ignites your players' imaginations, turning cautious strategy into wide-eyed dread and careful planning into frantic improvisation as they realize the battlefield has become a swirling maelstrom of imminent doom.

Miniatures are where the magic starts. There's something deeply satisfying about having a tiny, physical representation of your character and slamming it onto the table like you're declaring war. Moving a barbarian mini into position and growling, "I rage," hits differently when you have a visual and can actually see that tiny axe-wielding menace closing in on their unsuspecting target.

Hero minis bring your players' characters to life in a way words sometimes can't. If your players have a rogue who insists on doing everything in a shadowy corner or a paladin who poses dramatically every five minutes, having a mini that matches that vibe is sheer perfection.

Monsters deserve their moment in the spotlight, too. You don't need a mini for every single beastie that crawls out of the Monster Manual - unless you're swimming in a pool of gold like Scrooge McDuck and have the shelf space of a museum curator. Focus on the showstoppers: the boss monsters, the recurring villains, and the creatures you know will make your players mutter, "Oh no, not that thing."

For the rest - goblins, skeletons, the occasional pack of wolves - tokens, pawns, or even random household objects work just fine. Ever faced off against a fearsome army of bottle caps? Your players are about to.

And let's not forget the DIY approach because not all of us have a dragon's hoard of gold to spend on miniatures, and that's where that famous creativity kicks in. Coins, chess pieces, bits of Lego, or even jelly beans can stand in for enemies. There's something uniquely satisfying about defeating a troll and then immediately eating it in victory. Plus, nothing motivates a party quite like the thought of consuming their foes.

If you really want to take immersion to the next level and have the funds to match, 3D printing your own minis can feel like wielding a bit of arcane crafting magic. There's nothing quite like watching your players' eyes widen when you slap a freshly printed, fully painted dragon onto the table - a dragon you brought into existence, layer by painstaking layer.

But let's be honest, 3D printing is a pricey hobby that eats time and resin faster than a gelatinous cube devours adventurers. If the cost or the effort feels like too much, remember that there are incredible artists out there who've mastered the miniature-crafting arts, and they're more than happy to sell, or even gift you their work.

Supporting local artists or small online creators means you're not just getting beautifully detailed minis - you're investing in someone else's passion and keeping the tabletop community thriving. So whether it's a squad of goblins, a spectral lich, or a wizard who looks suspiciously like your best friend, find those makers who pour their heart into every print and let their creations help your world come to life.

Now, let's talk about maps. I've spoken about them in an earlier section, but there, I talked more about using maps as in-world artifacts while here, they have a meaningful purpose.

Maps are the unsung heroes of clarity. They stop your players from wandering off in the opposite direction because someone misheard 'east' as 'weast.' Battle maps are the backbone of any good skirmish - grid-based layouts where everyone can see exactly where they stand (literally) and just how many steps they are from certain doom.

Maps are powerful tools, and if you want to level up your map game, there's a whole world of cartography worth exploring. We've written a completely *free* guidebook that take a deep dive into this world - think dungeon blueprints, sprawling kingdoms, and fantasy maps that are so detailed they practically breathe.

Whether you're sketching by hand or plotting with digital tools, knowing about cartography helps you whip up maps that do more than just look pretty - they'll pull your players straight into your world and have them praising your artistic talent in no time. Even if you feel like your drawing skills are a lost cause, we'll take you through our step by step guide, turning you from Clueless Doodler struggling to hold your pencil, to Master Cartographer capable of creating stunning masterpieces.

Get your own free copy of the *Advanced RPG Cartography Guide* by scanning the QR code below, joining our mailing list, and unlocking the power to design your own battle maps.

But maps aren't just for battles. Even a hand-drawn sketch of a village, forest, or ominous dungeon can work wonders. It doesn't have to be a masterpiece; it just needs to give your players a general idea of where they are and where the likely danger is lurking. Trust me, a few wobbly lines and some labels like "Ye Olde Tavern" and "Definitely Not a Trap

Door" go a long way. It grounds your players, keeps the action focused, and gives everyone a sense of place without resorting to a 20-minute explanation that ends with blank stares.

And if you're playing online or just prefer digital wizardry, virtual maps are your best friend. Whether it's detailed dungeons, sprawling cities, or cursed forests, digital tools let you whip up visuals that look like you kidnapped a professional cartographer and forced them to work for dice and pizza.

With the right mix of miniatures and maps, your table stops being just a table and becomes a stage for epic heroics, ridiculous plans, and reckless sacrifices. Your players won't just imagine their journey; they'll see it, touch it, and maybe (if you've used jelly beans) taste it too. And honestly, what more could you ask for?

The atmosphere sets the stage, sure - the flickering lights, the eerie soundtrack, the adventurous snacks - but what really keeps your players at the table is what happens on that battlefield. No matter how immersive the vibe is, if your encounters fall flat, the session will fizzle out faster than a wizard's failed fireball. The real magic happens when you weave encounters that grip, challenge, and surprise your players, whether you've meticulously planned them out or whipped them up on the fly. Because let's face it: no one's really here for that glorified string cheese platter. They're here for the thrill of what comes next.

Balancing Prepared and Improvised Encounters

If your DMing skills are the soul, then encounters are the heart of the session. These moments of action, tension, and choice are what give your game its pulse. Whether it's a brutal showdown, a delicate negotiation, or a mind-bending puzzle, encounters drive the story forward. The trick is striking the perfect balance between carefully laid plans and on-the-spot creativity. Get it right, and your game stays sharp, thrilling, and just chaotic enough to keep your players on edge, eager to see what's coming next.

Prepared Encounters

Prepared encounters are your solid ground, your meat and potatoes, your "Yes, I actually did think about this ahead of time." These are the moments you've mapped out in detail, the NPCs you've carefully given tragic backstories to, and the challenges you've fine-tuned to be difficult but not so lethal that your players start giving *you* tragic backstories.

These are the moments you can supercharge with the right atmosphere - a haunting soundtrack, flickering candlelight, or even just the low hum of tension in your voice. Sure, you can sprinkle in this magic on the fly, but it

163 | Crafting a Great Session

really shines when you've prepped it ahead of time, fine-tuning every detail until it's a powder keg waiting to blow. Think of it like setting the stage for a play: every shadow, every note, every lingering pause, designed specifically to pull your players in, refusing to let go.

The goal of a prepared encounter isn't to railroad your players into one predictable outcome; it's to give them a strong foundation to jump off of and a clear framework to mess with.

When preparing an encounter, the first thing you want to ask yourself is: What's the point of this scene? Are you introducing a new villain who absolutely oozes malice and discontent? Testing the party's shiny new combat gear? Throwing them into an ethical blender of moral dilemmas? Or maybe just setting up a bit of comic relief to balance out the existential dread? Even if the point of the encounter is as simple as "give the rogue something to steal," "let the barbarian smash a goblin," or even "let the bard *smash* a goblin," there should always be some purpose anchoring the chaos.

Once you've nailed down the purpose, set the scene with a sprinkle of sensory magic and a generous helping of vivid imagery. Is the encounter happening in a dank cave where every breath tastes like mildew and bad decisions? Or maybe a bustling market where the smell of roasting meat competes with the clamor of bartering merchants and some suspiciously unsupervised livestock? (Don't forget to also add sound effects and ambient music to really drive this point home.) Just a few well-chosen details can transform a vague setting into something your players can feel. And if one of them decides to lick a dungeon wall for some godforsaken reason, well, that's on them.

But no good encounter is just a backdrop and a few witty quips. You need obstacles and stakes - the stuff that makes the scene pop. For combat, maybe the floor is riddled with unstable tiles, ready to collapse under the wrong footstep, or a lava pit that's just begging someone to slip and fall in. For a tense negotiation, maybe the NPC they're trying to persuade is one wrong word away from storming off in a huff. The stakes should be clear: what happens if they win, and what fresh hell awaits them when they screw up.

Now it's time to pick the enemies, challenges, or puzzles they'll face. Balance matters here - if your party of level three adventurers stumbles onto a dragon's hoard, there better be a compelling reason to run away screaming or a solid chance to talk the dragon into a lucrative side gig. The trick is to keep the challenge spicy enough to feel dangerous but not so overwhelming that the party collectively contemplates hanging up their adventuring gear.

And because your players are experts in smashing through your plans like toddlers through a Lego castle, always throw in a twist. Maybe the cultists they're fighting have a pet owlbear that charges in mid-battle, or the diplomat they're trying to win over is actually a doppelgänger who's been quietly judging their life choices. Twists make things memorable, and they give you that little glint of satisfaction when your players' jaws hit the floor.

Of course, rewards are the cherry on top. Give them something that feels earned, whether it's a treasure, a cryptic clue, or the priceless satisfaction of surviving your nonsense. And if you really want to mess with them, make the loot weird - a cursed dagger that whispers unsettling thoughts or a set of cultist robes that are suspiciously comfy.

Picture this: the party steps into a ruined temple, moonlight slanting through broken rafters, vines curling around shattered pillars. The floor looks ready to betray them with every step, and the air is thick with the scent of mold and the distant sounds of bats.

Ahead, a group of cultists mutter dark incantations while a shadowy figure in a hood orchestrates the ritual. The party's barbarian grunts, already cracking their knuckles, and the bard clears their throat for a one-liner. Just as the fight begins, the hooded figure glances up, and bam - the rogue recognizes their long-lost sibling under that sinister cloak.

The floor creaks ominously. The cultists hiss. The summoned shadow creature snarls. And your players? They're in it now. The stakes are high, the twists are twisted, and the rewards - well, that cursed dagger is practically begging to be picked up.

And there you have it: a prepared encounter with just enough structure to make it sing and just enough chaos to make it yours. Now let the players loose and watch them do what they do best - gleefully demolish everything you planned until you go insane.

Mastering Improvised Encounters

No matter how much you plan, no matter how tightly you clutch your lovingly crafted notes, your players will always find ways to surprise you. Maybe instead of battling the bandits you carefully balanced for an epic fight, they decide those bandits just need a little friendship and start sharing snack rations. Maybe they glance at the entrance of the dark, mysterious cave you've filled with puzzles, traps, and narrative significance and wander off to pet a nearby herd of goats because "they look friendly." Just like that, your carefully plotted adventure is now hanging by a thread.

But fear not - this chaos is the lifeblood of the game, and with the right attitude, you can ride the wave with style.

The first rule of dealing with player shenanigans is the same as the first rule of improv - say "yes, and..." When the rogue announces they want to seduce the ancient dragon you designed to incinerate them all in one fiery breath, don't shut it down. Lean in. Smirk, raise an eyebrow, and say, "*Yes*, the lady dragon is smitten by your proposal, *and* she plans to keep you around until you have your own special version of Shrek's Dronkies... whether you like it or not."

This isn't just an improv technique; it's your ticket to making the game feel alive, unpredictable, and ridiculously fun. Every wild plan they come up with - no matter how ridiculous or reality-breaking - is a door you can open to a new narrative. Sure, it might lead to a room full of chaos gremlins, but that's where the magic happens. Just be sure to give your players the consequences of their shenanigans as well. If that rogue tries to sneak away from that dragon, it *will* be a boss battle. And if your players decide to seduce those chaos gremlins? Well then, be ready for some chaos babies.

When you're improvising on the fly, remember the three critical elements: people, places, and problems. First, the people. Your mental library of NPCs is your best friend here. The next time your players ask, "Who owns this inn?" don't freeze. Just pluck someone off the top of your brain stack: "The innkeeper is Bruna, a no-nonsense dwarf with a deadpan delivery and an unhealthy addiction to terrible puns." Boom. They'll either love her or roll their eyes so hard they pull a muscle, but either way, you've got a scene.

Then, there are places. Even when your players yank the plot into uncharted territory, a few vivid details can anchor everyone in the scene. Maybe the inn smells like burnt bread and wet dogs. Maybe the mysterious forest is full of whispering leaves and judgmental squirrels. You don't need a whole Tolkien-esque description - just a few sensory hits to paint the scene.

And, of course, problems. Because what's a good improv scene without a challenge to mess things up? Maybe Bruna the innkeeper won't spill any secrets unless they best her in a pun-off, or the forest path is blocked by a very stubborn goat who demands payment in snacks. The stakes don't always need to be life-or-death; sometimes, the most memorable challenges are the ones that leave your players giggling or facepalming.

As a DM, you need to have fingers so fast they'd make a rogue's lockpicking look like knitting... for Googling references on the fly, of course. Do your players zig when you expected a zag? Do they demand the exact heraldry of a forgotten knight? Or do they fixate on the history of a cursed dagger you barely described? No problem. A quick tap-tap-search, and you've got the goods. Suddenly, you're delivering lore so rich it practically oozes with authenticity. The trick is making it seamless—like you've been hoarding that knowledge since the dawn of time and definitely didn't just scrape it from a wiki three seconds ago.

Remember those screens you set up for atmospheric lighting? Now they're pulling double duty. As your fingers dance across the keys, your screen lights up with a perfectly timed image - a grim, fog-choked fortress, a noble crest engraved on a rusted shield, or a dagger so cursed it practically bleeds malice. The players see it, and boom - your last-second improv becomes a cinematic reveal. They don't need to know that image was a frantic Google search; all they know is that you had the perfect visual ready to go. With the right picture at the right moment, you're not just making things up - you're weaving a world so vivid it feels like it's been waiting for them all along. Just make sure you avoid the photos with watermarks and low resolution; nothing kills your vibe quicker than the alluring nymph temptress you so perfectly described, popping up on the screen with a huge "Shutterstock" textbox that blocks out her features or an elven ranger NPC whose toned handsome face consists of at most eleven pixels.

But let's be honest: sometimes improvisation goes off the rails. Like, way off the rails. The kind of spiral where you're suddenly knee-deep in a debate with sentient mushrooms about municipal tax codes as the narrative slips into a fever dream.

When this happens, it's time to gently - or not-so-gently - steer things back toward sanity. Maybe as they argue with the talking fungus, a distant explosion shakes the ground. "Huh, weird. Wonder what that's about?" Boom. Instant hook. They'll catch the scent of the plot and dart back toward the main story - or at least toward something that doesn't involve fungal bureaucracy.

Of course, it helps to have a few safety nets for those moments when your brain sputters and the narrative engine stalls. Keep some random tables of NPC names, weird locations, and plot hooks tucked away like a secret stash of emergency chocolate. When in doubt, roll a few dice and let fate decide who they meet or where they end up.

It also doesn't hurt to have a few modular encounters in your back pocket - a bandit ambush, a traveling merchant with suspiciously cheap wares, a mysterious ruin that promises danger and disappointment. These little narrative nuggets can be dropped anywhere, like sprinkles on a chaotic cake.

And if all else fails, recycle. That spooky cave encounter they skipped last week? Slap a new coat of narrative paint on it and drop it into the next session. Your players will never know that the "abandoned watchtower" is just the last session's "ancient crypt" with fewer bats and more existential dread.

Remember, the chaos your players bring to the table isn't a bug; it's a feature. Every time they zag when you've meticulously planned a zig, they're handing you an opportunity to make the world feel alive and unpredictable. So embrace the madness, say "yes, and," and remember: when things get too weird, there's always a goat somewhere who can nudge them back toward the plot. Or, you know, bite them. You know how combative goats can get.

Managing Combat Immersion

Combat is the pulse-pounding centerpiece of a session, the moment when swords clash, spells erupt, and everyone at the table leans in with bated breath. But when combat drags, that pulse becomes the sluggish heartbeat of a dying campaign. Honestly, this is just plain hard because combat isn't just about swinging swords and flinging fireballs - it's a symphony of chaos where you're juggling initiative orders, enemy tactics, player abilities, and that one guy who keeps asking, "Wait, whose turn is it?"

It's keeping track of spells, hit points, positioning, and a half-dozen monsters who all seem to be plotting your mental downfall. And on top of all that, you're supposed to keep the atmosphere electric and the players immersed, all while having to do *basic math*! It's a lot. But here's the thing: when you nail it, when you ride that wave of tension and spectacle, it's *glorious*. So embrace the chaos, lean into the mayhem, and trust that when it all clicks, it'll feel like orchestrating the most beautiful, disastrous, unforgettable brawl ever.

Nothing shreds immersion faster than a fight that feels like it's being narrated by a sleepy DMV clerk or a player who zones out so hard they might as well be astral projecting. The key to combat that crackles with electrifying energy and unfathomable drama is keeping everyone invested, on edge, and maybe just a little bit scared for their characters' lives.

First things first: combat isn't just a series of numbers, dice rolls, and the monotonous exchange of "I hit it," "It hits you," on repeat until everyone's brain turns to pudding. No, combat is storytelling in its rawest, bloodiest form.

Instead of droning, "You hit for ten damage," paint the scene with a bit of flair. "Your sword slices through the goblin's patchwork armor, and it reels back, eyes wide, a spatter of blood marking its retreat." Suddenly, that goblin isn't just a hit-point sack; it's a desperate creature clinging to life.

And when the rogue delivers the killing blow, don't let it end with a mechanical shrug. "How do you finish it off?" Give your players the stage, and watch them transform a simple stab into a swan dive of death or a poetic flourish that would make a Shakespearean ghost weep.

When the dice gods bless someone with a crit or when a wizard unleashes a spell that could barbecue a dragon, give it the full blockbuster treatment. A fireball isn't just a math problem; it's an inferno that detonates with a deafening roar, heat waves blasting through the room, singeing eyebrows, and sending foes sprawling. Make those moments epic, like a fantasy film climax that spent the entire budget on sheer, jaw-dropping spectacle.

But no matter how vivid your descriptions are, if turns drag on like a snail through molasses, you'll lose that precious momentum. Keep it snappy. Give each player 30 seconds to decide their action - enough time to think, but not enough time to draft a dissertation on tactical warfare.

The key way of ensuring that players stay attentive is to ban phones at the table. I know, I know, it might be controversial, but if you can convince your players to do so, at least for the duration of combat, you'll have a much smoother session. "But I need it for my character sheet," your bard says through tears as you sassily point to the printer in the corner. Don't let your players fool you; remember you are the DM and, therefore, hold all the power.

Always, always remember cue up the next player. A simple "You're on deck, Steven" snaps everyone to attention. It's like an invisible cattle prod keeping the flow steady and the dread palpable. If someone's stumped, don't let the silence stretch into awkward infinity. A gentle nudge of "Want to ready an action?" can save the day and the pace.

Let's not forget the battlefield itself. If the combat zone is just a featureless void, you're robbing yourself of prime storytelling real estate, so make that environment work. Maybe the ceiling trembles ominously, chunks of stone start to dislodge, and suddenly, someone's rolling a dex save to avoid becoming a grease stain.

When the battlefield is alive, players start thinking beyond their character sheets. They're not just hitting; they're hurling enemies into walls, leaping onto tables, and using the terrain to turn a brawl into a set piece worthy of an action flick. And when they pull off something wild - say, kicking a bandit into a collapsing staircase or launching a goblin into a vat of conveniently placed boiling oil - it's a moment they'll remember long after the dice have cooled.

Combat should feel like a dance on the edge of chaos, where every swing, spell, and strategic decision pushes the story forward. Keep the descriptions vivid, the pace brisk, and the environment dynamic, and you won't just have combat - you'll have moments. Moments where the rogue's player screams in triumph, the barbarian punches the air, and the wizard cackles with the glee of someone who just turned reality into a special effects showcase. That's the kind of combat that doesn't just thrill. It burns itself into memory, one epic clash at a time.

Mixing Up Encounters

Combat is fun, no doubt about it - there's a thrill in rolling for damage, shouting dramatic one-liners, and imagining your character executing the perfect spin-stab of doom. But let's be honest: if every session turns into a relentless hack-and-slash montage, you're not running an adventure - you're running a medieval grind fest.

Eventually, even the most enthusiastic barbarian will start zoning out, and your rogue might wonder if their true talent is pickpocketing boredom. The trick to keeping things

175 | Crafting a Great Session

fresh? Variety. A glorious mix of role-playing, narrative-driven battles, and creative challenges that don't always require stabbing everything that moves.

First off, who said combat has to be a silent game of math and dice rolls? Inject some role-playing into those clashes, and suddenly, the fight isn't just about damage numbers - it's about drama, tension, and a little bit of sass.

Let the NPCs and enemies run their mouths mid-battle. A villain's sneering taunt of, "Is that pathetic swing really the best you've got?" can light a fire under your party faster than a fireball to the face. Or maybe the goblin being chased across the battlefield shrieks, "You'll never take me alive!" as the barbarian chucks his axe at him. That kind of banter gets players trash-talking NPCs (and maybe even each other,) fully immersing them in the scene.

And nothing spices up a fight like a good moral dilemma. Imagine mid-battle, a bandit drops to their knees, clutching their side, wheezing, "Wait! Spare me, and I'll tell you where the treasure is! It's under that weird whispering oak by the creek! The boss is just three goblins in a trench coat with a suspiciously fancy hat! And they argue all the time about who gets to be on top. The tavern keeper waters down the ale with swamp water, the blacksmith's been swapping good steel for shiny tin, and there's a necromancer in town who curses people's cutlery for fun. And if you find a talking map that insults your mother - that wasn't me; that's Barry the

Cursed Cartographer's doing. Please, I'll even tell you where I hid the cursed spoons I stole! I swear they were cursing me back!"

Sure, only about ten percent of that was helpful, but now your party has a choice: finish the fight or pause and negotiate. That's when things get juicy. Maybe the enemy recognizes one of the players. "I remember you from the war! You ruined my life!" Instant stakes, instant drama. Now that stabby rogue or broody fighter has a reason to hesitate, or better yet, a reason to fight harder. Suddenly, this isn't just another brawl; it's personal.

Combat also doesn't always have to be about wiping out every last enemy on the board. Give your players objectives that go beyond "kill everything." Maybe they need to protect a panicking VIP who has the survival instincts of a buttered potato.

Or perhaps the wizard is frantically trying to activate a glowing artifact while everyone else fends off a swarm of angry cultists. Maybe the goal is to snatch a cursed amulet from a lich's skeletal hands and escape before they become lich snacks. When the goal is more than just slaughter, combat becomes a frantic dance of priorities and strategy.

And if you really want to mess with your players' heads, throw in a dilemma that makes their swords feel a little heavier. What if their enemies are possessed villagers, unaware of their actions? Or what if stopping the villain means bringing down a building full of cockney, yet innocent, street urchin orphans?

Make them think twice before swinging. Watching your players grapple with moral consequences is its own kind of entertainment, and it makes victory taste that much sweeter - or defeat taste that much more bitter.

When things need a shake-up, let narrative combat step in to save the day. Ditch the rigid grid-based mechanics and let the story lead the way. Instead of tracking every five-foot step and angle of attack, loosen up and focus on the flow of the scene. Picture the chaos of battle: arrows whizzing overhead, swords clashing, spells bursting like fireworks gone rogue. "You charge through the fray, dodging wild swings and leaping over fallen enemies, your axe aimed straight at the necromancer's smirking face." It's fast, it's cinematic, and it keeps everyone glued to the action instead of their character sheets.

Highlight the big moments - the dramatic duels, the desperate last stands, the kind of clashes that deserve an over-the-top soundtrack and some slow-motion effects. Blend in skill checks to keep things interesting. "You want to vault over the table and tackle the cultist? Roll Acrobatics." When they succeed, describe it like an action hero montage. If they fail, let them faceplant spectacularly - failure is just an opportunity for slapstick heroics.

Contrary to popular belief, sometimes, the best combat is no combat at all. Who says every conflict needs to end in a pile of bodies? Set up skill challenges where players have to think their way out of danger. Maybe the cave is collapsing, and everyone needs to make frantic skill checks to leap chasms, stabilize a crumbling bridge, or spot the fastest way out before they get buried under tons of rock. Make escape feel like a fight against the environment itself.

Or turn a social interaction into a tense, dramatic encounter. Imagine the party trying to convince a paranoid noble to help them. Instead of rolling initiative, they're rolling Persuasion, Deception, and Intimidation. Every failure raises the stakes. Every success brings them closer to a fragile alliance - or a spectacular failure. The tension can be as tight as a drawn bowstring, but with fewer bloodstains to clean up afterward.

Let's not forget traps and puzzles, either, because sometimes, the deadliest enemy is a magical door that refuses to open until someone figures out a cryptic riddle or disarms a mechanism with more wires than a 90s bomb-defusing movie. Watching the rogue sweat over a ticking trap can be just as nerve-wracking as any duel, especially when the stakes are "disarm it or lose a limb."

The advice I've given you may seem hard and overwhelming, but the goal here is to achieve total dungeon mastery. The good news is that things can be built upon, and doing just one of these things is better than nothing. So, take it slow, keep building up your skillset, and before you know it, you will be a Supreme, Cool Ranch, Dungeon Master Taco.

You're standing at the threshold of true dungeon mastery, and yeah, it's a lot. No one said juggling combat, drama, and moral dilemmas while maintaining player immersion was easy. Keeping track of initiative, health pools, and who's about to get set on fire by a stray fireball is the mental equivalent of herding caffeinated cats through a hedge maze of catnip.

But here's the thing: every moment you keep the chaos contained, every time you spin that mess into an epic story, you're forging yourself into a sharper, deadlier DM. You're building muscle memory for drama, flow, and split-second decision-making.

When it feels overwhelming, start with one thing. Add a bit of banter to the next fight. Throw in a moral dilemma when they least expect it. Swap out a typical slugfest for a skill challenge. Take it piece by piece, scene by scene, and let your confidence stack like a barbarian's rage dice. Before long, you won't just be running combat - you'll be orchestrating cinematic, edge-of-the-seat, dice-clattering mayhem. And your players? They'll be there, week after week, ready to roll, shout, and scramble their way through the chaos you've crafted.

Variety is the key to keeping combat alive and your players on their toes. Mix it up. Let them fight, argue, negotiate, flee, or puzzle their way through danger. Because when the swords finally go quiet, you want your players to lean back, catch their breath, and say, "That was wild. What's next?" And you, grinning behind the screen, can just crack your knuckles and whisper, "Oh, you'll see."

Role-Playing Tips

Ah, finally we get to role-playing - the thing the whole genre is named after. Great role-playing is the spark that turns a decent session into a night of pure tabletop magic - the kind of night your group talks about for years, usually in loud, animated voices while someone waves a plastic sword around like an overly enthusiastic LARPer.

It's what takes the game beyond dice rolls and stats, transforming it into a living, breathing story where everyone at the table gets to be the main character of their own epic, ridiculous, and occasionally tragic tale. If you want role-playing that doesn't just shine but blazes with the intensity of a dragon's breath after it's eaten a particularly spicy goblin, then let's talk about how to make that happen.

First, let's deal with your NPCs. These are not just quest-giving vending machines or cardboard cutouts waiting to be looted. No, NPCs are the beating heart of your world, the people who give it flavor, chaos, and - if you play your cards right - a bit of emotional damage.

Give them voices. I don't care if you're no Matt Mercer; half the fun is in the effort. Maybe the innkeeper has a voice like they gargle gravel for breakfast and never, ever gets a name right. "Welcome back, uh, Gregorny. No? Geofforny? No? Whatever, you want ale or what?"

Maybe the ancient wizard ends every sentence with a triumphant "Aha!" like they just discovered the meaning of life, even if they're just telling you where the bathroom is. And if you're really feeling adventurous, throw in an NPC who speaks exclusively in metaphors that make no sense. "Ah, like a squirrel in winter, my friend, you must hide your acorns before the storm!" Will it be confusing? Absolutely. Will it be unforgettable? You bet your dice it will.

But a funny voice or a weird quirk is just the garnish. The real meat of a good NPC is their motivation. Even if they're just a humble carrot farmer, maybe they secretly dream of becoming a knight, wielding a rusted sword they found in a ditch, and practicing their battle cries when no one's looking.

When your NPCs want something - no matter how small or absurd - they feel real. They're not just there to hand out side quests; they're living their own lives with goals, dreams, and grievances that can bump into your players' adventures in unexpected ways.

Now, don't let these NPCs exist in a vacuum. Use them to hook your players into the world like a fisherman luring a particularly gullible trout. Connect them to your players' backstories.

Maybe the shady merchant at the crossroads isn't just any merchant; he's your rogue's old rival, still holding a grudge over that time the rogue swapped her wares for a sack of marbles and a kielbasa. Or maybe the healer in the village is the paladin's long-lost sister, who's been waiting for years to deliver a heartfelt monologue - or a slap to the face.

Having your NPCs remember stuff is a brilliant way to keep your players immersed. If the party saved the village from a marauding band of orcs, don't let the villagers just shrug and forget. Let them cheer when the party walks back into town, or give them free drinks.

Or if the party tried to rob the town blind, let the townsfolk tell their story. Let your players walk into a town expecting to be villanized only to realize the common people are having a festival in their name and getting drunk on Mudder's Milk in front of the party's surprisingly life-like statues made from mud.

These little touches make the world feel alive and responsive, and nothing gets players more invested than knowing their actions actually matter.

Of course, role-playing isn't just about the NPCs strutting their stuff; your players need to be in on the fun, too. Ask them questions that prod them to step into their characters' shoes. "What does your barbarian say to the terrified villager who just insulted his lack of hair?" "How does your wizard react to being called a hack by a rival mage?"

Give them opportunities to think beyond the mechanics and into the messy, glorious chaos of their characters' personalities. Sometimes, all it takes is a well-placed question to turn a reluctant player into an impromptu Shakespearean actor, waving their arms and dramatically declaring vengeance over a stolen loaf of bread.

And when they nail it - when the rogue delivers a monologue belonging in a soap opera, or the cleric comforts a grieving NPC with a sincerity that makes everyone go quiet for a second - reward them. Give out Inspiration Points, high fives, or just shower them with the kind of praise that makes them feel like the Oscar winner for Best Dramatic Performance in a Role-Playing Game. When players see that their role-playing is not just tolerated but celebrated, they'll be more willing to lean in, to take risks, to let their characters be bold, ridiculous, or vulnerable.

At the end of the day, great role-playing is about making the world feel rich, the characters feel real, and the table feels like a place where anything - no matter how dramatic, absurd, or tear-jerking - can happen. It's about embracing the chaos of personalities colliding, stories unfolding, and the kind of unpredictable magic that only happens when everyone stops worrying about "playing it right" and just plays.

Give your NPCs some quirks that make them memorable, anchor them to your players' backstories, and toss out the kind of character questions that get players thinking deeper. Something like, "Why does your rogue refuse to go near the old cathedral?" can unearth a whole subplot of betrayal and guilt, or even a mysterious fear of overly judgmental stained glass windows. Celebrate the moment a player answers with a line so sharp it cuts through the table's laughter and leaves a moment of stunned silence. Because when role-playing hits that sweet spot, you're no longer just rolling dice and moving minis; you're weaving a story that will be retold for years, and maybe even exaggerated to epic proportions. *That's* when you know your game has become a legend.

Conclusion: Setting the Stage for Magic

Where you should start is simple: set the scene with an atmosphere that grabs your players by the imagination and drags them kicking and screaming right out of reality. Light those candles, queue up a soundtrack that hums with tension or triumph, and let the flickering glow of a TV screen cast eerie shadows across the table.

It's not about throwing money at fancy props; it's about making the effort to blur the line between your living room and the world you've built. When they walk in and feel that shift - that moment where the mundane falls away - you've already won half the battle.

From there, balance becomes your best friend. The dance between preparation and improvisation is what makes a session legendary. Yes, craft your encounters with care, lay out stakes that matter, and script those NPCs who drip with personality. But when your players inevitably decide to chat up the bandit instead of stabbing him, roll with it. Have those Google fingers ready to conjure up last-second lore or visuals, and do it with the confidence of someone who definitely planned for this exact moment. Nothing sells the illusion of mastery like seamless improvisation that feels like destiny.

Combat is where things get gritty. It can be a pulse-pounding thrill ride or a quicksand slog, and the difference is in the details. Keep the pace sharp and the stakes high. Narrate with flair - make hits feel brutal, misses feel tragic, and crits feel like fireworks. Let the battlefield breathe with collapsing walls, slippery bloodstains, and ominous shadows that shift with every roll of the dice. And don't let anyone zone out; a simple, "You're up next" can yank a distracted player right back to the heart of the action. When combat feels like a cinematic climax, the energy becomes contagious.

But don't let every session become a hack-and-slash grindfest. Mix it up, throw in some moral dilemmas or quirky objectives that don't involve stabbing everything that moves. Let a fight hinge on whether the rogue can snatch a cursed amulet mid-battle or force your players to decide if they can live with defeating an enemy who's just a cursed street urchin. Keep them thinking, keep them guessing, and you'll keep them hooked.

Role-playing is where the magic truly ignites. Your NPCs aren't background props in the shape of characters; they're the lifeblood of your world, the ones who smirk, stumble, and sometimes break hearts. Give them voices, quirks, grudges, and goals.

Tie them to your players' backstories so that every encounter feels personal. Ask your players questions that pull them deeper into their characters' minds, and celebrate those moments when they lean in hard, delivering lines so good they linger in the air like smoke from a spent torch. When the whole table buzzes with story, when laughter and tension collide - *that's* the sweet spot.

Props, visuals, and snacks might seem like extras, but they're the secret sauce. A worn map, a cursed dagger in hand, or a well-timed "crit cookie" can elevate a moment

187 | Crafting a Great Session

from fun to unforgettable. Use your screens to flash images that make your world real, let the smell of beef jerky turn a mine crawl into a gritty expedition, and never underestimate the power of a prop duck turned oracle.

This isn't easy stuff. Crafting a great session is like juggling flaming knives while riding a plot-twist unicycle over a kiddie pool of alligators. But here's the thing: you don't have to master everything at once.

Start small.

Add a new layer of atmosphere here and a touch of improv finesse there.

Each session is a chance to level yourself up.

Before long, you'll be a level twenty DM, running games that don't just *tell* stories - but *become* stories. Your players will lean back at the end of the night, wide-eyed and grinning, and say, "That was incredible." And you, with a sly grin behind the screen, will know exactly what's coming next: more chaos, more wonder, and more of that tabletop magic only you can conjure up.

Chapter 5: Growth

So you've been behind the screen long enough to know the ropes, dodge the dice-throwing, and survive the sessions where everything goes gloriously off the rails. But here's the thing: being a Dungeon Master isn't just about surviving. It's about evolving, thriving, and gleefully watching your players walk straight into the narrative trap you've set.

That's why this chapter is all about leveling up - not your characters, not your NPCs, but you.

We're going to talk about the art of player communication - because running a campaign without clear communication is like herding cats with no plan, no patience, and no treats. Whether it's handling feedback (both the glowing praise and the "constructive feedback" that makes you feel like you were hit by a bus), navigating no-shows, or making sure everyone's on the same page

189 | *Growth*

during your fiftieth Session Zero, good communication can mean the difference between a campaign that sinks and a campaign that sings.

But growth isn't just about managing the players; it's about mastering the craft of storytelling itself. Do you want to go from being a competent narrator to a master storyteller who can spin plots so intricate they'd make a conspiracy theorist jealous? Well, we'll cover how to weave plots, evoke emotions, and pace your stories like you've got the ghost of Hemingway whispering in your ear. Because let's face it, anyone can say, "Roll to attack," but not everyone can make their players' palms sweat with dread before the dice even hit the table.

This is where we dive into the deliciously personal journey of developing your unique style. This is where you go from being "a good DM" to being the DM your players rave about, the one with a style so distinct they can spot it from a mile away. Whether you're a chaos-loving improv maestro, a worldbuilding architect, or a drama-fueled narrative weaver, we'll figure out how to refine your spark until it's a full-on inferno.

Growth as a DM isn't about being perfect - it's about being better, one session at a time. If you read this book carefully (as I trust you have), you've noticed that my personal style is to openly communicate with my players, no matter what. I understand that might not be everyone's cup of tea, but I feel it to be an invaluable tool. I'll teach you the extremes so you can find your own perfect balance. So, put a kettle on, boil a fresh cup of tea, and let's dish.

Player Communication

Player communication is the linchpin of every great campaign - though it often feels like you're trying to teach rabid hobgoblins to write perfect Elven. It should be what elevates your game from a chaotic free-for-all to a cohesive, character-driven legendary tale. But let's face it - communicating with your players can sometimes feel like reading an ancient, cryptic scroll, complete with holes, ink smudges, and vague threats of doom.

I learned this the hard way during one particularly cursed campaign, that the not-so-recent global pandemic forced me to run online. It started with the usual lineup of excuses: "Kids need help with homework," "Internet outage," and the classic, "My dog ate my character sheet." (Despite the sheet being online.) Those I can deal with. But that evening, mid-battle with a wyvern, the rogue just vanished. Poof. No explanation. Like Batman ghosting Commissioner Gordon. Everyone froze. The wyvern looked almost embarrassed to still be there.

After an awkward silence and a few half-hearted dice rolls, we called it early. The next morning, I got a text: "Sorry, fell asleep. How'd the fight go?" How did it go? Oh, we just tossed the wyvern a sandwich, gave it a pat on the head, and went home. Thanks for asking.

That was the moment I realized I needed a better system for player communication. Not just reminders or vague, hopeful check-ins, but real, structured ways to handle feedback, absences, expectations, and those one-on-one sessions that can turn a good campaign into something legendary.

Because when communication fails, it doesn't just derail a session - it can drain the fun out of the whole table. And to be honest, a table drained of fun is like a dungeon with no traps - sure, you're making progress, but where's the thrill of imminent doom?

To keep the wheels from falling off mid-adventure, let's tackle those communication pitfalls and fine-tune your table into a well-oiled storytelling machine. We'll talk about how to give and receive advanced feedback without anyone rage-quitting, how to handle the inevitable "real life" interruptions with grace (or at least minimal grumbling), and how to take the concept of Session Zero and crank it up to eleven. We'll also dive into the art of individual sessions - those glorious, character-focused side quests that make players feel like they're starring in their own fantasy spinoff.

If you've ever stared at a group chat filled with vague thumbs-up emojis and wondered if anyone actually read your message, or if you've had a player ghost mid-session because their pizza delivery took priority over the dragon fight, this chapter's for you. Because a campaign where everyone's on the same page - and maybe even excited to be there - is a campaign that's headed for greatness... or at least fewer wyvern-related awkward pauses.

From Feedback to Feast

Feasting on feedback is the art of transforming your players' vague affirmations of, "Ah, yeah, it was, like, *alright*," into actionable insights you can actually use. It's like plunging into an underwater sushi-fueled adventure, where instead of spearing fish, you're hunting for elusive feedback gems with the determination of someone who promises not to surface until they've hooked the catch of the day.

The goal isn't just to hear, "That fight was awesome!" but instead, dive deeper and fish out the right marine delicacies to help you spice up your campaign. We covered the feedback sandwich in our last book. You know, the classic structure of positive feedback, critique, and then positive feedback again to top it off.

It's 1 AM, and you need something reliable to fill that gnawing void in your stomach. The feedback sandwich is just that - simple, satisfying, and guaranteed not to upset anyone. You start with a compliment ("I loved the dungeon's atmosphere!"), slip in some critique like a pickle on a burger ("Combat felt a bit slow in the middle"), and finish with another positive ("But that trap at the end? Pure genius.").

The beauty of the feedback sandwich is that it cushions the critique between two layers of encouragement, making it easier to digest. The first compliment sets a positive tone, showing the player or DM that their effort is appreciated, while the final praise ensures the conversation ends on an upbeat note. It's not about sugar-coating criticism; it's about delivering it in a way that motivates improvement instead of crushing enthusiasm.

But sticking to the same formula can get stale. Have you ever tried to eat a sandwich for every meal? It gets old... Fast. Sometimes, you need to switch it up - add some spice, go for more detail, or sprinkle in real-time feedback to avoid the need for a huge intervention-style meeting at the session's conclusion. Tailor it to your players: some thrive on straight-shooting critique, while others need a bit of sugar with their salt. A solid feedback system keeps things fresh while leaving everyone satisfied, ensuring they're always hungry for more.

Taking Feedback with(out) a Grain of Salt
Getting feedback is one thing, but knowing how to implement it is an entirely different beast. Receiving feedback on your DMing can be a bit like cooking for a group of friends: you put your heart and soul into the meal, slaving over a hot stove all day, and then someone says, "You know, this is too salty." Ouch, your poor creative heart. But here's

the thing: as much as it may sting, without that feedback, you'd never know to put less salt in your sauce next time.

As the DM, your sessions are your recipes, and your players are your consumers. When your diners give honest, constructive feedback, that is not an attack but an invitation to make your dish fresher, more refined, and overall more palatable the next time you make it.

To successfully implement feedback, you must separate your ego from your work. And while that's easy to say, it's not always easy to do - trust me. When you've spent hours crafting an encounter or a plot twist, hearing it didn't land quite right can sting. But remember, feedback isn't a rejection of your effort - it's a reflection of how your players are experiencing the game.

You're not a failure if something didn't click; you're just a chef learning to season with the right amount of spice at the right time. When your players say something like "That combat dragged" or "It made no sense why the NPC did this," avoid defending or explaining. Do your best to instead listen and nod while mentally filing the critique under "Notes for Next Time."

Breaking down feedback is one of the best ways to apply it. Picture your session as a multi-course meal and your players' comments as specific tweaks for each dish. The pacing was slow" might mean adding more spicy moments like spontaneous ambushes, timed challenges, and sudden moral dilemmas - just to turn up the heat. "The NPCs felt flat" could entail giving each important character a strong defining quirk, goal, or backstory - a garnish that makes them shine.

Pinpoint the core areas of your game that need work, and try to improve them one at a time. Working on everything at once is like tossing a whole spice rack into the stew in one go. It's overwhelming, and although you may get lucky, it will often end in disaster. Your only hope at that point is a talking rat falling from the ceiling and fixing it for you. And when has *that* ever happened to anyone?

If you want your players to feel heard, show them you're acting upon their feedback. "Hey, since you mentioned last session's combat was slow. I tried to add more environmental hazards and a countdown this time. Let me know how it feels." Not only does this show your players that you care about their experience, but it also gives them a sense of investment. They're not just consuming the game; they're helping shape it by choosing their favorite seasonings. Do that, and the more your campaign improves, the more they'll appreciate your initial willingness to adapt and grow.

Of course, not all feedback is useful. Sometimes, a player's comment may be less of a "constructive critique" and more of a "random complaint about not being the center of attention." This is when you start to filter. If feedback feels like it's coming from a place of personal bias or doesn't align with the overall vibe of your group, don't sweat it. Not every suggestion belongs on your menu. Trust your gut, and know the difference between a helpful tip and an out-of-place gripe. At the end of the day, it's your game. Feedback can be great, but don't let yourself get stepped on. Finding balance is key.

Last but not least, remember that improvement takes time. Successfully implementing feedback is a process, and that process is eternally ongoing; it's not just a one-shot fix. Each session is another opportunity to hone, adapt, and get closer to becoming an enlightened DM. Think of it like fine-tuning a recipe: the more you tweak the ingredients, the better the dish becomes. But before you can cook up improvements, you need feedback in the first place. Not all players will hand it over on a silver platter. Some are too polite, shy, or just plain quiet. So let's explore some ways to gather those juicy insights, serve up the right questions, and create a feedback loop that keeps your game - and your players - thriving.

The Buffet Approach: A Spread of Questions

The buffet approach involves offering a vast selection of questions and letting your players pick what they want to comment on. Not everyone is ready to give a full Yelp review on demand, so give them options.

"What did you enjoy most about tonight's session?"

"What felt a bit off or could've used some extra spice?"

"Is there anything you'd like to see more of in future sessions?"

Think of these questions as different trays of food - some players will dive into the main course (combat and plot), others will nibble on the sides (NPC interactions or pacing), and a few might just go straight for dessert (the funny, epic moments).

This way, your players have a tasting menu of feedback options, and they can sample whatever feels most appetizing to them. No need for anyone to chow down on a full-course critique if they're not in the mood - they can just pick at the parts they're hungry to discuss. One player might take a generous helping of "That combat felt perfectly seasoned," while another might sprinkle in a little "That plot twist was a bit undercooked." It's feedback that goes down easy because it's served in manageable portions rather than one giant, indigestible lump.

Think of it like an all-you-can-eat conversation, where everyone can load up their metaphorical plate with precisely what they want to say. By giving them a spread of options, you're reducing the pressure and making feedback a relaxed, no-fuss meal.

Just like any good buffet, you'll get a mixed bag of tastes: the rogue thinks the dungeon was too spicy, the wizard wants a little more salt on the puzzles, and the bard is just thrilled the whole thing didn't turn into a burnt mess. It's low-stakes, high-reward, and guarantees you walk away with a flavorful blend of insights without anyone suffering feedback indigestion.

The Stir-Fry Method: Real-Time, Sizzling Feedback
The stir-fry method is all about keeping the feedback hot and spontaneous, like tossing ingredients into a sizzling wok. Instead of waiting until the session's over, try sprinkling in questions during key moments when the battle wraps up, when the players escape a trap by the skin of their teeth, or when an NPC interaction sparks laughter and confusion. Casually ask players for their thoughts right then and there, while the adrenaline, hilarity, or frustration is still fresh in their minds. Stuff like "Did that puzzle feel engaging and challenging, or did it need clearer clues?" or "Is this combat dragging, or are you all still invested?"

Quick, off-the-cuff questions keep feedback light, breezy, and immediate. You're not asking for a full magazine-style foodie review; you're just checking if the flavors are working mid-bite, like a waiter who always seems to check on your table while your mouth is stuffed full of food - but better because your players will actually *want* to be giving feedback.

For instance, if you see a party struggling over a door that requires solving a puzzle to open, and you see their faces scrunched in frustration, a quick, "Is this fun for you or do you just want to kick down the door and keep going?" can be life-saving. Admittedly, while this is a bit immersion-breaking if your players are already frustrated, sometimes breaking immersion is the lesser of two evils. They will appreciate it - and so will you.

I speak from experience. One time, I ran a session where I introduced a chase sequence - a dynamic rooftop pursuit through a bustling city. I was excited, and my players were excited, but midway through, I noticed everyone's enthusiasm starting to wilt. Instead of pushing through, I paused and asked, "Is this still fun, or do we need to speed things up?"

My rogue immediately chimed in with, "Honestly? This is starting to feel like when Dora the Explorer won't just look behind her as you scream at her through your screen." When I heard that, I immediately cut the sequence where they were running, and with their next jump, they were face-to-face with the big bad henchmen, ready for a showdown. Using the stir-fry method allowed me to get to the meat of things without making anyone suffer through fantasy cardio or annoying self explanatory Spanish lessons.

The Build-Your-Own-Burger Technique: Customizable Critique

Sometimes, getting useful feedback means letting your players choose exactly what they want to critique, like building a burger with just the right toppings. Offer core categories like "story progression," "combat intensity," and "NPC interactions," and let them stack their feedback however they want. "Rate tonight's session on these three things, and feel free to throw in any extra toppings."

Some players will pile their burger with plot feedback and a generous drizzle of NPC commentary, while others will go heavy on combat critique with just a dollop of story suggestions. Maybe one player tells you, "The story was a sizzling medium-rare, but the combat felt like soggy fries - no crunch, no excitement." Perfect. Now you know exactly where to add some seasoning.

The trick is to listen closely and ask follow-up questions to get specifics. If they say the combat lacked bite, ask what they'd prefer: more dynamic environments, higher stakes, or faster pacing. If the plot felt tremendous but the NPCs seemed bland, dig into what would make those characters more memorable - quirks, motivations, or maybe a weird catchphrase that'll haunt them forever.

Once you've got the flavors identified, don't let that feedback marinate too long. Implement small changes in your next session to see what sticks. If combat needed zest, try adding an environmental hazard or a twist mid-fight. If the story was perfect but NPCs needed work, introduce one with a personality that jumps off the plate - like a merchant who speaks entirely in riddles or a bard who thinks they're in a one-person musical. Just remember to take things slow and one at a time. Everyone loves a massive burger until they realize it's stacked so high they can't fit it into their mouths. Focus on adding one topping at a time until you hit that sweet spot, lest your players give up and start deconstructing your burger with a fork as you watch in mortified horror.

The Slow Cooker Method: Simmer Feedback Between Sessions

Sometimes, feedback needs a little extra time to bubble to the surface. That's where the slow cooker approach comes in - letting ideas and impressions simmer between sessions so you can check in when the flavors are just right. Instead of demanding immediate feedback while the dice are still warm, you let everything rest and give your players a chance to process their thoughts, as ideas gently percolate in the background of their brains.

A day or two after the session, send out a casual message to the group. Something simple, like, "Hey, thinking back on that last session, was there anything that really worked for you or anything that felt off?" It's low-pressure and lets your players respond when they've had time to mill over their experience. You might be surprised at what comes up. A player who was quiet at the table might suddenly unload about how much they loved the tense negotiation with that shady merchant or how the pacing of that dungeon crawl felt like a slog through molasses.

The beauty of this method is that it gives players the freedom to reflect, separate from the urgency of the moment. Some folks *like* slow-cooking stews - they need a bit of time before their ideas and opinions are ready to be served up. Give them this time, and they give you the most thoughtful, measured feedback.

After my last particularly convoluted mystery arc wrapped up, I gave it a few days to simmer before fishing for feedback. Mystery plots are like fine threads - you never know if your players are meticulously weaving them together or hopelessly tangling them in knots. When I finally asked how everyone felt, one of my most stoic players, the kind who typically offers feedback with a grunt or a single eyebrow raise, leaned back and smirked. "I gotta be honest. I'm pretty sure I missed that clue because I was too busy trying to get your kittens to stop attacking my shoelaces." The table erupted in laughter, and I couldn't help but grin as I glanced at the two culprits curled innocently directly next to (but not inside) the very expensive cat bed I bought them.

That moment was pure gold - funny, honest, and ridiculously relatable. It told me the mystery was compelling enough to stick with him, but my DMing style needed an adrenaline shot to out-compete my adorable yet devilish kittens. When you're up against cute animals, even the most crucial plot threads can get shredded, just like my couch cushions. It was a reminder that players are still human, vulnerable to adorable distractions beyond the realms of dice and dungeons. The story had hooked them, but next time, I'll be sure to check in more with those brave adventurers fending off adorable feline chaos.

This method also lets you fine-tune your follow-up questions. If you notice someone hasn't chimed in, a direct nudge like, "I'd love to hear what you thought about that big battle!" often gets the feedback flowing. It's like stirring the pot just enough to keep things from sticking.

So, be sure to let those thoughts simmer between sessions. A gentle check-in a day or two later keeps the communication going, ensures feedback is richer and more thoughtful, and saves you from those awkward, blank-stare moments when you ask, "Any feedback?" and hear only the chirping of crickets. It's slow, it's steady, and it keeps your game as flavorful as a perfectly cooked stew while also giving you the time you need as a DM to distance yourself from your work so you can more easily absorb the given feedback.

The Leftover Review: Let It Marinate

Sometimes, the best feedback isn't served fresh but is instead a leftover stew of thoughts and reflections. The Leftover Review is all about letting things marinate and then scooping out the juicy bits of feedback later - days, maybe even weeks after a session. Unlike the Slow Cooker Review, which simmers over texts and chat groups, this method is done face-to-face. Think of it as a variation of Session Zero.

Run a little Q&A session before you play as you pass around thoughts that have aged like fine wine (or, let's be real, like slightly stale pizza).

Here's how it works: you casually let your players know they can bring up anything from past sessions, with no expiration date required. Maybe you're all grabbing post-game tacos, or you've just finished another session, and everyone's in that loose, contemplative mood. You toss out a simple, "Anything still nagging you from the last few sessions?" and then let the conversation meander. The goal here isn't an immediate, laser-focused critique but more of an open invitation to air out lingering thoughts.

This method can be a double-edged sword, though. Letting players dredge up feedback from multiple sessions ago might feel like you're unearthing a crypt full of old grievances.

Suddenly, you're reliving that time you accidentally TPK'd them with goblins wielding suspiciously cohesive combat tactics or the moment they felt railroaded into fighting the Big Bad when they really just wanted to start a duck-farming empire. The danger is that it can derail into a greatest-hits reel of every minor frustration, leaving you wondering if your campaign is secretly a psychological endurance test.

But if you can ride the wave, the payoff is worth it. Sometimes, players need a little time to process the story, the stakes, and how they felt about their choices. Given space, they might realize that the twist they griped about three weeks ago was actually brilliant or that the puzzle they struggled with was challenging in the best way. You get the kind of reflective, nuanced feedback that only comes from time and perspective - the stuff that can transform a good campaign into a legendary one.

On the flip side, maybe a player who was upset in the moment has had enough space to cool off to turn his spice level eleven curry into an easier-to-manage three. Or a player who didn't have a problem with accidentally being pushed to the sideline for a single session but has begun to realize it is starting to happen more frequently. You can use this method to receive feedback that takes more than a single session to marinate. Like on leftover nights when there isn't enough of any one dish left, so they all get pulled out of the fridge and reheated, making your own little mini buffet.

This method also shows your players that the story isn't disposable. Their experiences matter beyond the session's end, and their thoughts can bubble up anytime. It creates a table culture where everyone understands that the adventure - and the feedback - can be an ongoing dialogue. Just be ready to balance the freedom with a bit of gentle steering. Let the feedback flow, but know when to close the lid and say, "That was last session's meal; let's focus on tonight's feast."

The Full-Course Critique: Deep-Dive Discussion
Every so often, it's worth doing a full-course critique - a dedicated sit-down where you go through the session piece by piece, from appetizer to dessert. This isn't just a casual, "Hey, how was it?" This is a structured review. Start with the opener (how was the session's hook?), move to the main events (plot, combat, major decisions), and finish with the sweet stuff (what made them laugh, cheer, or groan in that delightful "I hate you, but I love this" way).

For instance, after a big story arc concludes, gather everyone outside of game night for coffee or a Discord call. "Let's talk through the last arc - what worked, what didn't, and what you want more of going forward." Maybe they loved the creepy forest setting but felt the final boss fight was a bit stale. Or maybe that random NPC you introduced as a joke became their favorite part of the campaign (RIP Randy the Blacksmith - you were too pure for this world).

This kind of detailed feedback is gold, not just for tweaking future sessions but for figuring out what really makes your players tick. The downside is that the more detailed the feedback is, the harder it may be as the DM to accept. As a DM you're an artist, and getting critiques on something you are passionate about and dumped your soul into can feel like a swift punch to the gut. Do your best to step back and separate your emotions from the criticism. It's not easy, but it's your first step to fully utilizing the full course critique method.

Now comes the fun part: putting the feedback to use.

Take what they give you and start cooking. If they say the boss fight felt stale, maybe they were craving some environmental chaos - collapsing ceilings, rising lava, or a conveniently placed chandelier to swing on. If they loved the NPC shenanigans, lean into it. In the next session, throw in a few quirky side characters or give Randy's long-lost cousin a cameo. When your players see their suggestions woven into the game, it transforms feedback from a chore into a collaborative thrill.

And don't just focus on fixing things. Use the sweet stuff, too. If they say the session's tension was perfect, take notes on what built that tension: Was it the pacing? The ominous descriptions? The NPC's poorly hidden smirk? Those are tools you want to keep in your DM toolbox, polished and ready for next time.

The beauty of a full-course critique is that it keeps your campaign dynamic. You're not just running a story - you're co-creating an experience. And when your players feel like their voices shape that experience, they're more invested, more excited, and way more likely to stick around for the next wild ride you've got planned.

Feed Them and They'll Feed You

Getting advanced feedback isn't about grilling your players or forcing them to dissect every moment of the game. It's about keeping the conversation light, flexible, and - dare I say it - fun. Whether you're serving up a buffet of questions, stir-frying ideas on the spot, or letting things marinate overnight, the goal is to create a table where feedback flows naturally and everyone has a say in shaping the story. And remember, when all else fails, bribe them with cookies. Everyone talks more when there's a cookie in hand - it's just science.

Feedback is a two-way street paved with narrative gold, crunchy combat, and whatever zany NPC quirks you can dream up. Just like feeding your players snacks fuels their in-game decisions (and keeps the hangry pizza roll guzzlers at bay), feeding their desire for a great story with attentive, adaptable DMing means they'll dish out feedback that makes your game even tastier. It's a delicious cycle of creativity: the more they feel heard, the more invested they become, and the more insight they'll give you in return.

Every time you implement a player's suggestion - be it adding a morally gray villain, upping the ante in combat, or bringing back an NPC they weirdly adore - you're showing them that their voices matter. And that, my friend, is like giving them a seat at the head chef's table. They'll savor every moment of the story because they helped season it.

But this isn't just about you serving up improvements; it's about fostering a culture where feedback is expected, welcomed, and savored. Create an environment where players know their thoughts aren't just tolerated but treasured. When they see their ideas reflected in the next session, they'll keep coming back for seconds, thirds, ninths, and maybe even surprise dessert.

So keep those communication channels open, experiment with different feedback methods, and don't be afraid to ask for a taste test along the way. When you make feedback part of your game's rhythm, you're not just running a campaign - you're cooking up a collaborative feast that everyone wants a hand in making. And trust me, nothing tastes better than a story where everyone at the table helped stir the pot.

Once you've mastered advanced feedback and served up those juicy nuggets of player opinions, it's time to return to the kitchen and season your next Session Zero to perfection - because a well-marinated start makes the whole adventure taste better.

Session Zero to the Nth Degree

Ah, Session Zero. The sacred prelude to a campaign where hopes are high, dice are yet to be rolled, and everyone's still pretending they'll show up every week on time like responsible adults.

You've got your group assembled, character sheets crinkling, and a unfounded sense of optimism that no one's going to derail your meticulously crafted plans before you've even started. But this isn't just any Session Zero. We're going to kick this baby into high gear, crank it up to a level that would make Spinal Tap proud, and lay down the kind of groundwork that could support a wizard's tower made entirely of multiverse-threatening misfires.

Let's start with a little thing I like to call the campaign primer. This isn't just some snooze-worthy syllabus of "We'll be playing in the Forgotten Realms, and I expect a 10-page thesis on Elvish genealogy by Tuesday."

No, this is your campaign's mixtape, your cinematic trailer, your chance to say, "Hey, here's a taste of what's to come. Buckle up, buttercups." This is the place to drop hints of the big themes, like, "A demonic plague is spreading, and no one knows why," or "The gods have abandoned the world, and everyone's spiraling into existential dread."

Throw in some tantalizing hooks, weird NPC teasers, and maybe a line like, "The fate of reality hinges on the exalted one who controls the last remaining enchanted ham sandwich." Whatever gets your players leaning in with a spark of curiosity in their eyes. If your primer doesn't leave them itching to roll dice and make bad decisions, rewrite it until it does.

Now, tone. Imagine your campaign as a blockbuster movie. Who's directing it? Are we talking Spielberg-level epic quests with tear-jerking heroics? Or are we going for a Tarantino-style blood-soaked flick with non-linear chaos and morally dubious monologues? You may even want to channel some *Monty Python and the Holy Grail* energy, where every victory is met with absurdity, and someone inevitably gets turned into a newt that says Ecky-Ecky-Ecky-Ecky-Pikang-Zoom-Boing-Gumzowehzeh.

Establishing this directorial tone during Session Zero means everyone's on the same creative wavelength. It avoids that awkward moment three sessions in, in which the rogue believed they were in a gritty noir thriller, but the bard's been roleplaying their character like it's an episode of *Adventure Time*.

Speaking of characters, let's get visual. Sure, your players can say their barbarian is "big and scary," but wouldn't it be better if they specified that the barbarian looks like Jason Momoa had a love child with a grizzly bear?

Encourage your players to draw inspiration from celebrities for their character's appearance, voice, or even *both*. Maybe the paladin talks with the stoic gravitas of Keanu Reeves in *John Wick*, or the wizard has the unsettling monotone of Tilda Swinton explaining existential dread. This isn't *just* for fun; it also locks in the necessary mental images and makes role-playing more vivid. When someone says, "I glare at the innkeeper like Tommy Lee Jones in *No Country for Old Men*," everyone knows exactly what kind of energy is being served.

But it's not all cinematic fun and games. We also need to talk about safety tools because nothing kills a vibe faster than realizing half the table is uncomfortable with that surprise torture scene you thought would be a fun plot twist.

Before you hurl your players into chaos, you need to establish comfort boundaries because nothing shatters immersion faster than realizing your "fun twist" is making half the table squirm. That's where lines and veils come in. Think of lines as hard "nope" zones - topics that are completely off-limits, like violence against children or body horror. Veils are more like "fade to black" moments - the content exists, but we skip the gory details. For example, a romance scene gets a simple "You spend the night together" instead of a play-by-play. Of course, if your party is ok with any of these things, go for them; they can make a game more fun - in *lots* of ways. But these are some good common areas you should check in about.

During Session Zero, ask your players what's a line and what's a veil for them. It's like setting the movie rating for your campaign so everyone knows the boundaries. And remember, these can shift mid-game - if someone's uncomfortable, pause, adjust, and move forward. A table that feels safe is a table where everyone's free to dive in, drama first, no hesitation.

Think of it like deciding on pizza toppings. Everyone loves pizza, but someone's bound to veto anchovies. Respect the veto, because forcing anchovies on someone is punishable by jail time. The goal is for everyone to have fun, not to make them wonder if they'll need therapy because of your next plot twist.

Once you've laid down these ground rules, it's time to heat things up. One of my favorite advanced techniques for Session Zero is what I like to call the prequel montage.

Instead of just talking about character backstories, try role-playing out a few key scenes. Maybe the rogue and the bard meet in a shady tavern, attempting to con the same mark. Maybe the cleric has a vision from their god that sets them on their quest as the warlock lurks in the shadows, debating whether to eavesdrop or order another drink.

These little snippets give players a chance to feel out their characters and test their dynamics, maybe even forming alliances or rivalries before the main campaign kicks off. It's like the first ten minutes of a Netflix show where you're already hooked before the title screen even drops.

You can let players role-play these scenes or describe them themselves. If they're shy or unsure, step in and use their backstory to narrate a defining moment that shaped their fate or brought them to that seedy tavern where destiny (and the rest of the party) awaits.

Of course, I wouldn't be giving quality advice if I didn't share a cautionary tale. During one of my early campaigns, I underestimated the power of a well-run Session Zero. I figured, "Eh, we'll just wing it and figure things out as we go."

Well... We winged it alright, and... Yeah... we did *not* figure things out...

The chaotic evil rogue kept stealing from the party because "that's what chaotic evil rogues do," the lawful good paladin was outraged at the lack of morality, and the wizard was too busy studying his tomes (scrolling Instagram) to notice the brewing chaos.

By then, we'd spent more time arguing about character motivations than actually adventuring. It was like watching a poorly written reality show where everyone secretly hated each other. The lesson here? Set expectations early, or risk turning your campaign into *The Real Housewives of the Forgotten Realms*.

Lastly, use Session Zero to review scheduling, commitment, and what happens when someone inevitably flakes. We all know life happens, but setting clear expectations up front - like "If you miss three sessions in a row, we're turning your character into an NPC who sells questionable potions in a back alley" - keeps everyone on the same page.

Believe me, it's better to have these conversations now than to deal with the fallout when Greg suddenly vanishes mid-campaign and takes the only healing spells with him.

Players Missing Sessions

How many times have you received the dreaded message: "Hey, sorry, I can't make it tonight." No phrase strikes more fear into a Dungeon Master's heart. Sure, it's just one player, but the domino effect has begun. The carefully balanced encounter, the NPC's dramatic reveal, the entire session hinged on this person being there, and now they're off the grid like a rogue avoiding their tab at the tavern.

So what's a DM to do? Start weighing your options. And like everything in this glorious, chaotic hobby, each option comes with a catch - or at least a cautionary tale.

Rescheduling is the first solution that pops into your mind. It's fair, right? Everyone gets to be present, and no one misses out on the epic twists or the boss fight you've been teasing for weeks. It seems like a diplomatic choice. So you take a breath, open the group chat, and type, "No worries! How's next week?"

Well, now you've unleashed the beast. The collective calendars of your players are like an eldritch puzzle, constantly shifting and impossible to solve. One person's available on Thursday, another's busy with a "work thing" on Friday, someone else has a birthday dinner on Saturday, and, inexplicably, the druid is MIA on Monday because of their weekly knitting circle.

You shuffle dates like a time wizard, desperate to align five people for one night of make-believe. The next session slides back a week. Then another. Suddenly, two months have passed. The once-hot anticipation of the campaign has cooled to a lukewarm shrug.

If you think that's an exaggeration, let me tell you about "The Eternal Scheduling Saga." What was supposed to be a gritty, low-fantasy survival story turned into a tragicomedy of Google Calendar invites. We rescheduled six times in a row. Six! Somewhere between the third and fourth attempt, hope died, but I kept up the facade, messaging the group with forced enthusiasm: "We'll get there, guys! The band's still together!" But the band was not together... The band was sliced into chunks, strewn across the ruins of my sanity. Eventually, I looked at my notes, sighed, and realized the campaign was over - not because the players weren't interested, but because our collective schedules had slain it like a vengeful paladin smiting a particularly annoying necromancer.

Of course, rescheduling can work now and then, but if it happens more often than playing, it's time to cut your losses and push the campaign forward.

But what if there's just one player missing? Believe it or not, the solution is relatively simple, albeit a tad ruthless. Just play without them. The story has to keep moving, or it risks fossilizing. Sure, it might feel a little harsh, but if someone's constantly absent, it's better to accept reality and let the party continue the quest. Besides, if they're a reasonable human, they'll understand. And if they're not - well, dodging that drama is just another form of party survival.

So, you've chosen to leave them behind; all you have to do now is work it into the story. When a player ghosts the session, and there's a big showdown coming, you've got a decision to make. It's like standing in front of three doors in a dimly lit dungeon, each one offering a different way to handle the absence - none of them perfect, but all of them workable.

The first door? The good old handwave. This is the quick-and-dirty fix, where you declare that the missing character is off in the background doing something useful, but generic, like guarding the rear, keeping watch, or contemplating the deep mysteries of life while everyone else gets their hands dirty. It's simple, efficient, and doesn't slow the game down.

But do it too often, and the character starts to feel like Captain Marvel - someone who just happens to always be busy during the crucial moments. Nobody wants to come back and find out their legendary paladin spent three sessions pretending to be a hallway decoration.

Then there's the second door, where you pass the reins to another player. Hand over the absent character's sheet and let someone else take a crack at it. This is like lending your friend a prized weapon - but there's trust involved that they won't mess it up by trading its life for a handful of magic beans.

It's a solid option if the party needs that character's abilities to survive, like the healer keeping everyone on their feet or the rogue disabling a trap that's just begging to ruin someone's day. The trick is making sure the stand-in knows to respect the character's usual vibe.

If your stoic wizard suddenly starts juggling fireballs and flirting with goblins, you're setting yourself up for an awkward conversation later. Lay down a few ground rules: no weird decisions and no wild detours. This works best when your group knows each other well and respects each other's characters. If there's even a whiff of doubt or if you think the missing player would be peeved someone else took their character for a spin; there's always the third door.

And that third door? That's when you, the DM, take the wheel. You know the stakes, you know what plot twists wait around the corner, and you know that the rogue vanishing mid-combat makes about as much sense as a dragon hoarding socks instead of gold. So you just... run the character yourself.

Keep it simple and functional - no Shakespearean monologues or hero moments, just enough action to keep the gears of the story turning. The barbarian swings their axe, the cleric mutters a healing spell, and the ranger loses an arrow or two. It's like guiding a borrowed cart down a narrow path: careful and deliberate, with an eye on avoiding any spectacular crashes.

After the session, let the player know what their character did. Transparency is key unless you want them to return to a bizarre new reality where their bard now owes a life debt to a squirrel.

The main downside of this door, of course, is that you have one extra thing to balance as the DM, which can be tricky, especially if you are beginning to implement the new tips and tricks from this book. Filling in for someone once isn't a huge deal, but once it becomes a habit, it may be time to go back to discussing consequences for missing a session and if your players are genuinely respecting your time.

Ultimately, whichever door you choose depends on the situation and the chaos levels of your table. If it's a low-stakes session, handwave it and move on. If the party's survival hangs in the balance, delegate to a trusted player. And if the plot is balancing on a knife's edge, take control yourself to keep things from spiraling into the void.

The goal is to keep the adventure rolling, the party functioning, and the story full of life. Because while one player might be absent, the quest waits for no one. Choose your path, open the door, and embrace the glorious mess that follows.

Of course, sometimes you can simply leave the character missing for most of the session, but then you need to explain the absence in a way that makes sense to the world. Maybe the ranger went on a solo hunting trip, the cleric got summoned by their deity for some urgent celestial paperwork, or the bard got a doctor's note to excuse him for the day.

It's simple, it's clean, and it doesn't require you to do narrative gymnastics. Just keep it light. The party doesn't need a three-act drama to justify why Carl the Wizard isn't here; a one-liner about him getting food poisoning from the local tavern stew will do just fine.

And hey, if the missing player throws a wrench into your plans for the night and you're not in the mood to improvise around a phantom character, there's always the backup plan: spontaneous game night! Keep a few board games handy for these moments. Maybe bust out *Betrayal at Baldur's Gate* for some chaotic fun, or if everyone's feeling too emotionally exhausted to strategize, declare it a *Lord of the Rings* Extended Edition marathon. Nothing says "we're still having fun," like enthusiastically telling your players, for the fifth time, that Viggo Mortensen *actually* broke his toe in that scene while you eat snacks meant for a boss battle that never happened.

But what if everyone but one person cancels? The table's empty, your snacks are lonely, and your carefully crafted session is left hanging like a cliffhanger with no resolution. It's tempting to rage-quit the night and drown your sorrows in pizza rolls, but wait - opportunity knocks.

This is the perfect chance for a solo session. Maybe the rogue gets a secret side mission, the warlock deals with their patron's latest unreasonable demand, or the fighter goes on a personal quest to reclaim their honor (or their favorite drinking mug). Individual sessions breathe life into character arcs and set up future drama for when the whole party returns.

Individual Sessions as Canon Events

Whether it's a solo side quest or a deep dive into a character's backstory, one-on-one sessions have the potential to add rich, gooey cheese layers to your campaign lasagna.

However, running a game for just one player can feel like juggling flaming swords while blindfolded. Without the buffer of a full party, the spotlight is blindingly bright, and the pressure to deliver is higher than a wizard's stress levels during finals week at Hogwarts.

Fear not, brave Dungeon Master, for with the right approach, you can turn these intimate sessions into unforgettable sagas instead of painfully awkward improv exercises.

First things first, consider the power of NPCs to fill in the gaps left by the absent party members. You don't need to create an entire company to tag along with your lone adventurer, but a couple of well-crafted NPCs can work wonders.

Think of them as supporting actors in a buddy-cop film - each with their own quirks, skills, and occasionally inconvenient personal dramas. A snarky thief who owes too many people too much money or a loyal knight who takes everything way too seriously can balance the dynamic beautifully.

These NPCs not only provide mechanical support in combat and exploration but also create opportunities for banter, drama, and emotional gut punches. Nothing says "memorable session" like an NPC clearly designed as comic relief suddenly delivering a tearful speech about the nature of sacrifice.

To make these NPCs shine, focus on their personalities and motivations. Don't just slap a stat block on them and call it a day. Give them goals, flaws, and an annoying habit or two. Maybe the thief mutters insults to themselves when they fail a pickpocket attempt, or the knight insists on reciting their family motto before every battle. These little details make the NPCs feel alive, making them feel like real people instead of like convenient plot tools for the players.

They can challenge the player's decisions, provide moments of levity, or even become unexpected scene-stealers. I once had a rogue's shady NPC sidekick trip over a barrel during a stealth mission, leading to a chaotic domino effect of mishaps. The player laughed so hard they almost choked on their soda, and that NPC became a beloved fixture of their solo escapades. It's these unpredictable, human (or not-so-human) moments that breathe life into your story.

If NPC party members aren't your jam, lean wholly into the solo experience by crafting a journey that's all about your player's character. A solo session is the perfect chance to dig deep into their backstory, motivations, and personal demons.

If they're a brooding ranger haunted by their past, send them on a mission that dredges up old wounds and forces them to confront their fears. If they're a bard who thinks life is just one big tavern song, drop them into a situation that tests their charm, wit, and ability to talk their way out of a literal dragon's den. And if they're a barbarian who believes every problem is a nail waiting for their hammer, toss them into a diplomatic meeting where smashing things is technically off the table - but the table itself is surprisingly fragile.

The goal is to make the session feel like a spotlight episode of their favorite show, where every twist and turn is tailored to them. They should walk away from the table feeling like their character grew, struggled, and maybe even achieved something they never thought they could in a group session.

You might need to crank up that player's power level for that session so they can feel like John Wick on a solo mission. Most TTRPGs are balanced for a full party (not one relentless force of nature plowing through enemies), so you'll have to fine-tune things so they can shine without breaking the game. Just be sure you properly communicate and justify the temporary buff so the player doesn't ask where his bullet-time crossbow went the next time you play with the whole group.

One of the biggest advantages of solo sessions is the freedom to explore plot points that might derail a full-group campaign. In a regular session, if one character suddenly decides they need to visit their long-lost mentor or avenge their family goat, the rest of the party might start eyeing the clock or quietly scrolling through memes. But in a solo session? The whole narrative bends to their whims.

The lone adventurer can have heart-to-heart talks with NPCs, explore hidden locations, or follow bizarre clues without worrying about holding anyone else up. It's like a custom DLC for their character's story - exclusive content designed just for them. This is your chance to make them feel like the main character of their own epic saga, complete with dramatic confrontations, moral quandaries, and maybe even a tearful reunion or two.

Of course, even the best solo sessions can veer into "Wait, what do I do now?" territory if you're not prepared for the unique challenges. The most important thing is to keep the tension and stakes high. When it's just one player, there's no safety net of party members to bail them out, so the danger feels more immediate.

If they're sneaking through a cursed temple, make every creaking floorboard feel like a potential death sentence. If they're negotiating with a shady crime lord, crank up the paranoia until they're sweating bullets.

Without the chaos of a full party to distract them, every decision feels more impactful. That intensity is what makes solo sessions so special. There's nowhere to hide, and every success - or failure - rests entirely on their shoulders.

When the party bails and only one player shows up, panic becomes a real and immediate companion. There was no way I was canceling on Tyler; the guy was already on his way (plus, he helped me move the weekend before, so I owed him one). So there I was, staring at his character sheet like it held the secrets of the universe. Tyler's rogue, Vax

Blackwhistle, was a scam artist with a penchant for small-time cons. Perfect. I could work with that.

With about ten minutes to spare, I scrapped the grand story arc and spun something out of desperation. Enter Drakeshore: a grimy port town where trust goes to die and opportunity smells like low tide. As Tyler arrived, confused he was the only one there, I had just enough of a threadbare premise to pretend I'd planned this all along.

Vax slipped into the market, eyes sharp, searching for a mark, and I dangled a puffed-up noble in front of him like bait on a hook. Overdressed, overconfident, and stupid enough to trust a rogue. He offered Vax a "business opportunity" - a mysterious crate to be picked up at midnight on Pier #7. I didn't know what was in the crate yet, or what I would do if he asked about the other six piers, but who needs details when you have adrenaline-fueled improvisation?

Midnight came. Tyler rolled for stealth and nailed it - Nat 20. Vax peeked into the crate, and inside... a chicken. Just a chicken. My brain came up with that on the spot and started melting because I couldn't figure out what to do next, but the show had to go on. So, I leaned into the absurdity. As Vax returned to the noble, Tyler didn't miss a beat; his rogue spun a tale of doom and destiny, proclaiming the chicken to be Cluckthulhu, the feathered harbinger of the apocalypse.

The noble went pale. His confidence evaporated, his curlicue mustache drooping in fear. He paid Vax a sack of gold just to escape the "curse." And because I apparently thrive on my own chaos, the chicken laid a golden egg right there in Vax's hands.

Tyler's eyes lit up. Vax left the pier richer, with a doom-chicken sidekick named Sir Pecks-a-Lot and a story that had spiraled completely out of my control.

That's the magic of solo sessions born out of desperation. It wasn't polished, it wasn't planned, but it was alive. And all I had to do was cling to Tyler's character concept and sprint alongside the chaos.

Running a session for one player is like baking a personalized cake. You want it to be rich with flavor, tailored to their tastes, and sprinkled with just the right amount of danger. Use NPCs to provide companionship and chaos, or let the solo adventure shine by diving deep into their character's soul. Keep the stakes high, the story personal, and be ready to roll with the weird choices they make.

And if all else fails, remember: you can always have them hit the villain in the boing-loings and scamper away into the night. That's the kind of spontaneity that makes one-on-one sessions legendary. Whether it's a solo escapade or a group catastrophe, every session is an opportunity to spin a tale that your players will never forget - and that's where the real magic of becoming a master storyteller begins.

Becoming a Master Storyteller

Let's level up your storytelling skills so you can go from being a DM who tells a story to a master storyteller who spins tales so immersive your players feel like they've stepped into their own personal fantasy movie - except there are more critical failures and you have the budget of a college theater department (you'd think that'd mean high but... it's low... shockingly low... like unfathomably low).

Non-Linear Narratives: Messing with Time Because You Can

A non-linear narrative means telling your story out of order - think of it as shuffling your campaign timeline like a deck of cards and dealing out scenes in a random order.

You can drop your players into a tense showdown only to jump back and show how they got there. Picture them standing in a burning village, swords drawn, eyes wild with panic.

Then you hit pause and rewind: "Six hours earlier, everything was calm... too calm." It's like showing them the fallout before they even know what transpired. This approach injects instant intrigue and keeps players hungry to connect the dots.

They're not just on a journey - they're unraveling a mystery wrapped in time loops and narrative breadcrumbs.

Think of *Pulp Fiction* and your sheer joy of realizing how those seemingly disjointed threads eventually tied together.

You meet Vincent and Jules wiping brains off a car window before you know who the poor guy in the backseat is.

That same thrill applies to your campaign. Maybe your players defeat a villain early on, but only later do they learn they've been dancing to his schemes all along. Done right, non-linear storytelling transforms your campaign into a puzzle where the satisfaction comes from snapping each piece into place.

Just remember: keep track of the timeline like your sanity depends on it (because it does), and make sure the payoff is worth the head-spinning. Your players should feel like they're in on the greatest twist ever - not tossed in a blender of plot confusion.

In a campaign, maybe you drop your players right into the middle of a dungeon fight with no context. One minute, they're trading blows with a slime-covered monstrosity, and the next, you hit them with, "Three days earlier, you accepted a very questionable job offer from a man in a cursed cloak." It's like handing your players a puzzle where half the pieces are missing, and the picture on the box spontaniously bursts into flames.

I once ran a campaign where I decided to steal... borrow, a narrative trick right out of a Hollywood blockbuster: putting the big boss fight in Session One. No buildup, no ominous foreshadowing, just an immediate plunge into chaos.

The party opened with a brutal, bone-rattling brawl against a lich they'd never seen before. This wasn't your standard "mosey into the tavern and hear rumors of evil" setup. No, these poor souls were knee-deep in necrotic energy with a skeletal sorcerer cackling in their faces before they even knew each other's full names. Swords were drawn, spells flew, and they barely scraped through the encounter by the skin of their teeth - bruised, bewildered, and with just enough hit points left to squeak out, "Why DM? Why?"

That's when I hit the pause button and flipped the script. The next few sessions rewound the clock, shifting into a series of flashbacks that pieced together how they got there in the first place.

One session, they were rescuing a scholar who had a dangerous obsession with ancient artifacts. Another, they were exploring a forgotten crypt where the air reeked of old magic and bad decisions. Each flashback revealed a thread of the larger story, a breadcrumb trail leading them inevitably back to that first harrowing clash with the lich. They met NPCs who'd go on to betray them, stumbled upon clues they hadn't understood at the time, and made choices that sealed their fate. Every revelation felt like a gut punch wrapped in an "Ah-ha!" moment.

It was storytelling Jenga - pulling blocks from the middle of the narrative stack and hoping the whole thing didn't come crashing down. But man, it worked. When the timeline finally looped back around to the boss fight, the players weren't the same wide-eyed adventurers who'd stumbled into that lich's lair. They were ready. They knew what was at stake, why it mattered, and what they had to lose.

This time, they charged in with purpose, fueled by vengeance, redemption, or just the desperate need to not repeat that last bone-chilling encounter. And when they finally took the lich down for good, the victory tasted sweeter because they'd earned it twice over - once in battle, and once through the unraveling of their own story.

Non-linear storytelling didn't just make the fight memorable; it made the entire journey feel like a puzzle worth solving. The players weren't just experiencing a tale; they were assembling it, piece by piece, until the whole, glorious picture came into focus. And honestly, isn't that what makes a great campaign? Not just the fights and the wins but the realization that every moment - past, present, and future - fits together to form an epic campaign they'll spin yarns about for ages.

Multiple Perspectives: Everybody's Got a Story to Tell

Multiple perspectives are all about showing the same event through different NPCs' eyes. It's like *The Usual Suspects*, where everyone's version of the story is skewed by their own biases, lies, or conveniently selective memories. This is fantastic for making your world feel alive and messy - because, let's face it, everyone's the hero of their own tale, even a lowly NPC.

Picture this: the party saves a town from rampaging bandits. The mayor sees them as noble heroes, the local merchants think they're opportunistic mercenaries, and the bandit leader swears they're heartless villains who steal candy from babies *for fun*. Now your players are walking around town with three different reputations, wondering if they're beloved, feared, or just that weird group that nobody wants to sit next to at the tavern.

I once had an NPC blacksmith named Jeremy whose shop was robbed. He described the thief as "a towering brute with arms like tree trunks." Another NPC - an old bard with a penchant for exaggeration - swore it was a shadowy figure who "melted into the night." The thief turned out to be a halfling rogue with a bad attitude and worse stealth skills. The players had a blast unraveling the conflicting stories, mostly because they spent an hour trying to figure out how a "towering brute" could leave halfling-sized footprints.

Chekhov's Gun: If You Plant It, Make It Go Boom

The principle of Chekhov's Gun is simple: if you introduce a loaded gun in Act One, it better go off by Act Three. In your campaign, this means every detail you sprinkle in - no matter how trivial - should eventually lead to a moment of revelation or consequence. If your players pick up a rusty key in Session Two, by Session Ten, it should open a door that unleashes a long-buried nightmare or reveals a trove of treasure glimmering in the dark.

Maybe that key unlocks a cell where a vengeful specter has been imprisoned for centuries, ready to haunt the party's every step. Or perhaps it leads to a hidden vault piled high with riches that hint at a forgotten kingdom's downfall. The payoff can be dread or delight, but it needs to land with purpose. If the key never turns a lock, it's just dead weight. And in storytelling, dead weight drags the momentum down like a stone tied to an adventurer's ankle.

But what if the gun doesn't go off? That can work, too - if it's intentional. Maybe the loaded gun sits on the mantle the whole campaign, a silent threat, a ticking clock that never chimes. The key they found rusts away in their bag, and when they finally remember it, the door it was meant to unlock is long gone.

These moments can drive home themes of lost opportunity, fate's cruel humor, or the chaos of adventuring life. Just make sure the silence of that "unfired" gun is loud enough to be meaningful. If it doesn't go off, it should still feel like it matters, like the players chose to leave that thread dangling - or fate yanked it away.

One time, I casually mentioned a creepy, moth-eaten tapestry in a decrepit castle. The players, naturally, ignored it because they were too busy looting everything that wasn't nailed down. Twenty sessions later, when they needed a secret passage, guess what was behind that tapestry? The collective groan of realization was the chef's kiss perfection.

Foreshadowing: The Art of Planting Landmines of Suspense

Foreshadowing is all about dropping subtle hints about future events. It's like sneaking spoilers into your campaign without anyone noticing. Remember how, in *Breaking Bad*, random glimpses of a charred teddy bear hinted at the chaos to come? Do that. Drop symbols, recurring motifs, or cryptic prophecies that make no sense now but will hit like a truck later.

Maybe the party keeps seeing murals of a shadowy figure holding a shattered crown. They think it's just ancient decor until they realize they're about to shatter a kingdom. The best part of foreshadowing is when your players look back and say, "Wait... you were warning us this whole time?" Yes, yes, I was, and you didn't listen. Delightful.

One time, in a sprawling high-fantasy campaign, I planted a seemingly innocuous detail in the very first session. The party arrived in a bustling port city, and as they wandered through the cobbled streets, they noticed an old beggar with a rusty music box. The tune though beautiful, was hauntingly strange, and the beggar mumbled something about how "the song's gonna play at the end, whether you're ready or not." The players wondered what he meant by "the end" but ultimately just shrugged, dropped a copper piece into his cup, and moved on to more pressing matters, like arguing with a fishmonger about the price of suspiciously sentient-looking clams.

For the next ten sessions, the music box's tune would pop up at random: a child humming it in a distant village, an eerie echo in a forgotten cave, a bard plucking the melody absentmindedly in a crowded tavern. Sometimes, they would notice and shrug, and sometimes they flat-out ignored it.

Then, during the climactic battle against a cursed warlord, everything clicked. The warlord's armor was shattering, dark magic crackling around him, and as he let out a final, chilling laugh, the rusty music box tune played from nowhere. The ground trembled, and the beggar's words echoed in their minds: "The song's gonna play at the end, whether you're ready or not." The warlord wasn't the end - he was harboring an ancient curse that wasn't going to die with him. The music box wasn't a quirky background detail; it was a ticking clock counting down to the curse's release and the subsequent existential threat to the whole world.

Cue the party's collective jaw drop and frantic scramble to figure out how to stop a full-on musical apocalypse. The landmine of suspense detonated perfectly, and as they desperately tried to seal away the curse, one of them muttered, "We really should've listened to that beggar." Indeed, delightful.

Subverting Expectations: Because Predictable is Boring

Nothing keeps players on their toes like a good old-fashioned expectation subversion. You set up a classic trope, then yank the rug out. Maybe the creepy old hag in the swamp isn't an evil witch but a retired paladin who bakes incredible pies. Maybe the kindly innkeeper is the villain pulling the strings. Just remember: subversion works best when it's earned, not just for shock value.

In one of my campaigns, the party spent days planning to fight an "ancient dragon" terrorizing a village. The party had spent real-life hours preparing for the ultimate showdown - villagers whispering about an ancient dragon, the barbarian sharpening his axe, the wizard scribbling contingency spells, and the rogue plotting more escape routes than actual combat strategies. Tension simmered, weapons gleamed, and they marched into the cave, ready to face fiery doom.

Instead, they found a baby dragon wailing over a lost shiny rock. The rogue sighed, took the rock he acquired randomly a few sessions ago out of his pocket, and held it out. The dragon snatched it, cooed happily, and flopped over, purring like a scaly kitten. The party exchanged sheepish looks, half-relieved, and half-mortified that they'd nearly declared war on a tantrum-throwing toddler. They left the cave, weapons sheathed, egos bruised, and returned to the village with their dignity barely intact.

Sometimes, subverting expectations means realizing your epic battle plan was just advanced-level babysitting prep. Just be sure to throw them a bone and let them describe to the mayor how "oh so scary" the encounter was so they still get paid.

Collaborative Storytelling: Give Them the Steering Wheel (Sometimes)

Finally, let your players in on the storytelling action. Collaborative storytelling means giving your players the power to shape the world. Let them invent factions, create legends, or add bits of lore. Not only does this lighten your mental load, but it also invests them deeper in the story. You're no longer the sole architect; now, you're co-creating a universe filled with unexpected twists, bizarre side quests, and lore so rich it could be bottled and sold as fantasy syrup.

If a player says their character once trained under a reclusive sword master who disappeared mysteriously, guess what? That sword master is now a plot hook. Maybe that missing mentor left behind a cryptic map scrawled on the back of a tavern menu. Maybe rumors swirl about a "phantom duelist" whose signature move mirrors the one your player just used. Your job is to take these little nuggets and let them explode into gold-mining opportunities for story depth. It's like improv: you build the world together, and the story grows in directions no one expected.

I once had a player declare that their bard had a "nemesis" who stole their song lyrics. That random tidbit turned into a whole subplot where the party tracked down the musical thief and faced off in a bardic duel akin to the shave contest scene in *Sweeny Todd*. I didn't plan it. I didn't need to. The players wrote the story themselves, and it was glorious chaos.

Another time, I had a player decide on a whim that their warlock's patron communicated solely through riddles delivered by enchanted carrier pigeons. It seemed like a one-off joke until, mid-session, a pigeon burst through a window with an ominous riddle about the town's mayor. Suddenly, the party was knee-deep in a political conspiracy that spiraled out of control faster than the pigeon could coo its goodbyes. Another time, a rogue claimed they were once part of the infamous Midnight Claw thieves' guild - an organization I hadn't even heard of until they uttered it. Three sessions later, the entire party was infiltrating a Midnight Claw hideout, dodging traps, and arguing with an overly enthusiastic parrot who thought it was their new guild master.

So, unleash your imagination, grab your dice, and remember: you're not just telling a story - you're orchestrating a living, breathing epic where everyone gets a front-row seat... including you. When your players throw curveballs, catch them and throw them back twice as hard. When they build the world, let them build. Because the greatest campaigns aren't the ones where the DM steers the ship solo; they're the ones where everyone's got a hand on the wheel, ready to sail straight into whatever storm of creativity you conjure up together.

Developing Your Own Unique Style

Your DMing style isn't just the way you run a game - it's the fingerprint you leave on every session. It's the moment players realize exactly who's pulling the strings behind the screen and brace for impact. It's the tempo of your plot twists, the flavor of your worlds, and the energy you unleash when the game hits its stride. Finding that style isn't just choosing a label and sticking to it; it's about discovering what makes your storytelling tick, then cranking that dial until the knob rips off.

Maybe you're a chaos-loving improv maestro, reveling in unpredictability. Your sessions are wild, frantic, and just on the edge of spiraling into beautifully orchestrated madness. NPCs pop out of thin air with motives even *you* weren't aware of five minutes ago. Plots twists and turns occasionally tie themselves in knots that you gleefully refuse to untangle. You prep just enough to light the fuse and watch the fireworks (or maybe dynamite), confident that whatever bizarre choice your players make, you'll ride the wave with a grin and a half-formed plan.

Perhaps you're a worldbuilding architect, sculpting realms so intricate they could be published encyclopedias. Your maps sprawl like tangled roots, and every city has customs, legends, and old family feuds. There's a depth to your world that makes even the background scenery feel significant. Every crumbling ruin has a story, every holiday festival a hint of ancient history. Your challenge isn't creating the lore - it's knowing when to reveal it. Sprinkle those details like breadcrumbs on a winding trail, just enough to keep your players hungry for more without choking them on exposition.

Or maybe you're a drama-fueled narrative weaver, spinning character arcs and emotional gut punches like a playwright with a penchant for pain. Your stories are built on tension, betrayal, and those moments that make the room go silent. You thrive on slow-burn reveals, moral dilemmas, and the kind of victories that come with a cost. But even in the most intense narrative, remember to balance the heartbreak with moments of absurdity. Because after all, what's a tragic hero's journey without an embarassing faceplant or two?

But here's the secret: you don't have to choose just one style. Blend them like a chaotic potion master or switch between them on the fly. Maybe you're an improv maniac who weaves surprisingly coherent lore out of spontaneous nonsense. Maybe you build worlds with the precision of a cartographer but let plot threads unravel into delightful chaos. Maybe your drama is carefully constructed, but you're always ready to toss in a wild, unscripted twist just to see what happens.

Don't be afraid to experiment. Run a session where everything is improvised - no notes allowed. Design a dungeon so rich with lore that it feels like it belongs in a museum. Push a plot twist so dramatic it leaves a ripple of stunned silence at the table. Stretch the boundaries of your comfort zone until you discover a blend that just *feels* right. The kind that makes you lean back with satisfaction and think, Yeah, that one's me.

Most importantly, trust yourself. Your style is forged from the stories you love, the games you've played, and the sparks that fly when you're deep in the zone. When you find it, you'll feel the rhythm of your game fall into place, unmistakably, undeniably you. And that's when the magic truly begins.

Conclusion: Beyond the Final Roll

The final session's echoes fade away - the clatter of dice, the whispers of schemes half-unraveled, the gleam of a hero's blade hanging in the dark. And in that fading, there's a lingering spark, like the last ember of a fire refusing to die.

Your table is a theater, your story a tempest, and you, Dungeon Master, are the storm-wielder. You are the whisper behind the shadowed curtain, the hand that threads fate and folly into a braid of wonder. With every tale spun, you are both architect and arsonist, building worlds only to set them ablaze with chaos and chance.

Growth isn't just the dust you shake off with experience; it's the flame you stoke, the roots you send deeper and deeper into the earth. Every player's laugh, every groan of despair, every wide-eyed silence is a piece of your evolution. You sharpen your craft on the whetstone of every misstep and triumph, honing it until it gleams like a blade waiting to be drawn.

This journey doesn't end at "good enough." It pulses forward, like a heartbeat under armor, urging you to explore new realms of storytelling, new depths of player connection. You will falter, you will rise, and you will spin the wheel again, daring fate to land where it may.

So gather your maps, your plots, your chaos - but most of all adventurer, gather your courage. Step behind that screen, knowing you are not just guiding a game but shaping an experience. An experience that lives eternally in the minds of those who journey with you, long after the torchlight fades.

And when the table falls silent, and the adventure's dust settles, let that silence be a promise: you'll be back, wilder and wiser, ready to weave the next unforgettable storm.

Chapter 6: Ending

Congratulations, you magnificent ringmaster of chaos. You've juggled plots, wrangled unruly players, and somehow navigated a campaign that felt like corralling cats with a laser pointer during an earthquake. And now, here you are, staring down the grand finale. The final curtain call, the last dramatic flourish, the moment where all those wild threads you've been dangling in front of your players either tie together in a beautiful knot or explode like a badly cast fireball.

But hey, you didn't come this far just to trip at the finish line. This is your chance to land the story in a way that leaves your players cheering, gasping, or maybe tearing up just a little (because of the story... not the pizza rolls you burned... *for the third time*).

Whether you're unleashing the final boss, crafting an epilogue, or setting the stage for future adventures, this is where you put the cherry on top of your campaign sundae. So let's make sure it's the kind of ending that everyone remembers - the good kind, not the "What the hell is even that?" kind. Hone your notes like daggers, summon NPC voices from deep within that reverberate like war drums, and carve the final pieces of story into legend.

The Final Boss

The air hangs heavy, thick with the kind of dread that sinks into your lungs and makes every breath feel like a risk. You're at the yawning mouth of the cavern now, where shadows cling to the walls like ancient secrets, and the smell of something long-forgotten curls up from the depths. You know what waits ahead.

Every choice, every gamble, every hard-won victory has steered you to this jagged threshold. Inside, the final boss lies coiled and patient, a storm wrapped in malice. You can almost hear their breath - slow, deliberate, like a predator deciding when to pounce. The torchlight sputters, barely holding back the dark, and beyond it, the unknown infinite expanse. This isn't just a fight. This is *the* fight, the one that'll etch itself on your memory whether you walk away victorious or tragically fall into legend.

Your party stands at your back, their faces stern with the gravity of what's to come. The rogue's fingers dance over their blades, eyes scanning every inch of the dark like it might betray its secrets. The wizard grips their staff like it's the only thing keeping the universe in order, whispers of spells slithering through clenched teeth. The barbarian rolls their shoulders, a smirk twitching at their lips - the kind of smirk that says they're ready to meet whatever doom has been promised. No more plans. No more doubts. You step forward, the crunch of your boots against stone sounding like the ticking of a countdown clock. The air shifts, colder, tighter, like the cave itself is holding its breath. Then, from the abyss ahead, a voice drips out - slow, venomous, and far too pleased.

"I've been expecting you."

The ground under your feet feels thinner now, as if one wrong step could crack the world in half. The end is here. You've run out of road. All that's left is to fight - and to hope that when the dust clears, your story isn't over just yet.

The final boss is the ultimate showdown where your players should feel like every decision, every triumph, and every absurd bit of party-inflicted chaos has led to this moment. This is where you pull out all the narrative stops, set the stakes so high they're scraping against the clouds, and make sure that everyone at the table knows - this is it. This is the crescendo, the fireworks finale, the emotional mic drop.

The first step is setting the mood long before they enter the boss's lair. Your players shouldn't stumble into the final confrontation feeling like, "Oh cool, another room with a conveniently evil person standing in it." No, they should feel the gravity of what's about to go down.

Maybe they've spent the last session unraveling dark omens and chilling prophecies. Perhaps NPCs they've come to care about deliver solemn farewells or make desperate last-minute requests. The world should start to feel heavier - like reality itself is holding its breath.

Don't just tell them the stakes are high; show them. If they're about to face the necromancer who's been raising an army of skeletons, let them see villages already crumbling and the air crackling with malevolent energy. If they're about to throw down with a tyrant king, make sure the battlefield is littered with the desperate hopes of those who need them to win.

This is where the stakes aren't just personal-they're world-shaking. Lives hang in the balance. Their triumph heralds salvation, but their downfall will unleash hellish annihilation.

And now, the moment you've all been waiting for... let's learn to perfectly craft the mastermind behind the mayhem: the Big Bad, the BBEG, the *villain*! This isn't the time for a cookie-cutter antagonist with a generic monologue. Your final boss should be personal. Maybe this is the warlord who torched the rogue's hometown, the ashes still clinging to their boots. Maybe this is the twisted mentor who shattered the paladin's faith, betrayal etched into their soul. Maybe this is the eldritch nightmare that's clawed nightly through the wizard's dreams, its whispers promising madness with every breath.

The very best final bosses aren't just challenges but emotional landmines that bring out the absolute worst and best in players. Give your villain a chance to talk. Let them gloat, let them taunt, let them reveal that last, terrible secret that makes your players' eyes widen and their knuckles tighten around their dice. The villain's words should have the party's blood boil or their hearts sink - preferably both.

Once the fighting starts, it's all about setting a scene that feels like the climax of a blockbuster movie. Describe the arena with cinematic flair. Perhaps they're standing on the edge of a volcano, molten lava splashing up like furious geysers. Maybe they are in a crumbling castle where chandeliers crash to the floor and lightning lights up the storm outside. This is not the time for subtlety; go big, go bold, and make sure your players can see the chaos, hear the roar of the battle, and feel the weight of every decision.

As the fight unfolds, let your players shine. This is their moment to unleash every spell they've hoarded, every combo they've theorized, and every reckless plan they've been dying to try.

Encourage their heroics. Let the barbarian hurl themself across the abyss, muscles straining and gravity be damned.

Let the cleric summon a divine smite that crashes down like a vengeful star, blazing with righteous fury. Let the rogue slip from shadow to shadow, a ghost of vengeance, plunging a dagger deep into the villain's spine as a victorious smile curls on their lips. And if they have to go out? Let them go out in a blaze of glory that is so epic that it makes the afterlife seem like a well-deserved nap.

And if someone dies - because let's be honest, final boss fights can be a meat grinder - make it count. Don't let them just keel over quietly. Give them a moment, a scene where they deliver a last, defiant one-liner or pass the torch to another player with their final breath. Let it be tragic, heroic, and, above all, memorable. Deaths in a final battle shouldn't feel like punishment; they should feel like legends in the making.

As the battle reaches its climax, keep the tension high. Make it feel like victory is hanging by a thread - one wrong roll, one misstep, and it all crumbles. But when they finally deliver that killing blow, make sure it lands. Describe the villain's downfall with all the drama you can muster.

"The necromancer's magic unravels in a violent explosion of dark energy. The tyrant king falls to his knees, the crown rolling away, lost to the dust."

Give your players the satisfaction of knowing they did it. They've triumphed. They've survived. They've won.

After the dust settles and the villain's corpse (or remains, or disintegrating essence) lies still, take a beat. Let the silence stretch. Let your players breathe in that moment of victory, that realization that the fight is over. The stakes were at their highest, the tension at its peak - and they came out the other side. Whether they're battered and bruised or victorious and glowing, let them savor it.

The final boss isn't just about delivering a challenging fight. It's about giving your players the climax they've earned - a fight that's thrilling, personal, and epic enough to be worth every moment of the journey. This is their story's peak, their chance to be the heroes they always knew they could be. So let the stakes rise and the emotions soar, and when it's all over, let them bask in the glorious chaos they helped create.

Epilogue

The final boss has fallen, the dust has settled, and the echoes of that last epic clash are fading into memory, and now your players are probably high-fiving, wiping away tears, or stress-eating the remainder of those burnt pizza rolls. But before you all pack up the dice and untangle yourselves from the narrative web you've been weaving for months or years, there's one last thing to do: the epilogue.

This is where you give your campaign the send-off it deserves - a final curtain call that wraps everything up and leaves your players knowing their characters' stories truly meant something.

Now, I know what you're thinking: "Didn't we already end the campaign? The villain's toast, the world is saved, we did the thing!" Sure, you could technically leave it there. But an epilogue is the cherry on top of your narrative sundae. It's where you give your players a chance to see the ripples of their actions. How did they change the world? Where do their characters go from here? How do they mourn the fallen?

What does "happily ever after" (or "sadly ever after") actually look like?

Think of it like the closing montage at the end of an adventure movie. The heroes ride off into the sunset. The rogue becomes a local legend, known for stealing hearts and wallets in equal measure; the wizard opens a school where the tuition is high, and the student mortality rate is higher; the barbarian retires to a quiet village where they smash barrels for fun, just in case one of them may be a mimic.

You're offering a glimpse of life beyond the campaign, a reward for the players' dedication and chaos-infused creativity. The trick is to make it feel earned and personal. Don't just dish out generic "you lived happily ever after" fluff - tie it to their character arcs.

If the cleric spent the whole campaign questioning their faith, maybe their epilogue shows them founding a new order based on what they learned. If the barbarian's life goal was revenge, maybe we see them finally laying down their weapons, their anger satisfied, ready for a peaceful life of, I don't know... goat herding? Everyone needs closure, even if it comes in the form of a barbarian trying to keep goats from escaping while reminiscing the time with his friends spent smashing things.

You don't have to write a novel for each character's fate. A couple of vivid sentences can be enough. Just imagine yourself as the narrator in a documentary about these brave, occasionally reckless adventurers. "And so, the bard returned to the tavern circuit, spinning tales of their deeds, embellishing liberally, and collecting free drinks from anyone who believed them." Boom - a perfect, cheeky send-off.

Let your players contribute, too. Ask them how they see their character's story ending. This isn't just your story; it's their story, too. Maybe the rogue wants to settle down and open a bakery with suspiciously good security. Maybe the paladin retires to a quiet village, only to realize that "quiet" and "village" are concepts they will never fully understand. Let their imagination run wild and fold it into the closing scene.

But the epilogue isn't just about individual endings; it's also about the world they leave behind. What's changed? If they saved the kingdom, did it rise like a phoenix from the ashes, rebuilding stronger than before, or is it now a bureaucratic nightmare full of paperwork about "proper dragon containment protocols"? Maybe the defeat of the villain has created some sort of power vacuum, and now a dozen would-be warlords are circling the throne like vultures around a fresh corpse. Show the world's response to your triumphs and failures, and let the world breathe a little as you close the book.

And for both Odin and Zeus' sake, if there is a dangly plot thread, just tie it off. If there's some mysterious figure who's been lurking in the shadows the whole campaign, give a hint as to who they were or what they wanted. If the bard made a deal with a devil way back in session two, let them reap the consequences. No one likes leaving the table with a nagging, "Wait, what about...?" rattling around their brain.

The epilogue, at the end of the day, is your last chance to do right by the journey you all took together. It's a way to say, "Look how far we've come.". Look at what we did." Whether it's bittersweet, triumphant, or laced with just the right amount of sarcasm, a good epilogue sends everyone away with a sense of closure - and maybe, just maybe - the tiniest hint that the adventure isn't really over. After all, in this game, it never really is; it's just sitting there, waiting for that next roll of the dice.

How to Conclude an Entire Campaign

Ending a campaign is like closing time at your favorite bar. You're not just shuffling people out the door; you're giving them a chance to finish their drinks, tell a few last stories, and maybe even sing a slurred rendition of *Bohemian Rhapsody* - complete with guitar solos, of course. A good campaign conclusion should feel like that - a final hurrah where everyone gets a moment, the lights dim just right, and the door clicks shut behind them with a sense of satisfaction.

Let's get one thing straight: wrapping up a campaign isn't about tying every plot thread into a neat, pristine bow. This isn't *Downton Abbey*. Some threads will be frayed while others will dangle off the edge of reality like a confused bard looking for their lost lute, and that's okay. What matters is that the important arcs get closure.

The rogue finally tracks down the treasure that's been haunting their dreams. The paladin resolves that festering moral dilemma that's been turning their alignment chart into an existential crisis. Your job is to ensure your players' choices had weight and their struggles meant something.

I once ran a campaign where, despite the looming prophecies, the tangled politics of warring kingdoms, and the constant threat of the world teetering toward ruin, my players chose to cling to a single, baffling mystery. Was it the fate of an ancient artifact or the true identity of a shadowy villain? No, it was something far more evil - a quirky, unexpected thread they picked up in session three and refused to let go. Every twist in the plot, every grand reveal, only served as a backdrop to their private obsession, a question they returned to with relentless curiosity and humor.

So when we reached the final session, standing on the precipice of fate and world-altering decisions, they weren't holding their breath to resolve cosmic conflicts or centuries-old secrets. It wasn't the unraveling of ancient prophecies that gripped their attention - it was the reveal of what happened to that infuriatingly unforgettable talking goat I mentioned so briefly in the first act. To say this destroyed me would be an understatement, but, of course, the show must go on.

So I gave them an ending where they stumbled upon a goat-owned tavern called "The Bleating Heart." Everyone lost their minds. They laughed, they cried, and one player actually made a reservation for their character's retirement party there. Closure doesn't always have to be grand; it just has to pull the correct emotional string.

Speaking of emotions, don't be afraid to sprinkle a bit of sentimentality into that last session. Yes, even if your campaign has been a wild carnival ride of chaos and bad decisions. After all the dice-fueled mayhem, sometimes the most powerful way to end things is with a quiet moment. Maybe the party gathers around a campfire one last time, the flickering flames reflecting off their dented armor and slightly traumatized expressions. They share stories of the time the bard accidentally seduced a gelatinous cube or the time the cleric rolled three natural 1s in a row and barely lived to tell the tale. These moments don't just wrap up the adventure; they remind everyone why they came along for the ride in the first place.

While you're at it, make sure to give each character a final victory lap. Let the wizard finally solve that riddle that's been gnawing at them for months. Let the barbarian beat someone in arm wrestling without accidentally flipping the table. Let the bard finally get a standing ovation that isn't from a room full of angry skeletons. This is their moment to shine, to strut offstage with all the confidence of a rogue who just rolled a natural 20 on Stealth and knows it.

After that, just wrap it up, raise a glass, and let them walk out of your world, knowing they left a few glorious, hilarious, and mildly scorched footprints behind. And when they ask, "What's next?" just smile and say, "Oh, you'll see."

Is This the End?

The credits are about to roll, and everyone's packing up their dice, already planning their next snack raid, but here's the thing: nothing ever truly ends. Not in a good TTRPG universe, anyway. The story might be over, but the world? The world is still out there, ticking away, full of possibilities, unanswered questions, and probably a few unsupervised magical artifacts just waiting to ruin someone's day.

If you want to keep the story going, you absolutely can. Here's how to make it happen.

Think of it like a good TV show finale. Sure, the main plot is wrapped up with a bow (possibly singed, because your party cannot resist setting things on fire), but you've left just enough dangling threads to hint that another adventure is lurking around the corner. Maybe the last scene shows a mysterious figure retrieving the fallen villain's cursed crown. Maybe the party's bard hears whispers of a new threat in a distant land, right before they hit the tavern stage for their next big gig. Maybe, just as the world seems at peace, a distant explosion reminds everyone that peace is more of a temporary suggestion than a permanent state.

You want to end with that perfect balance of satisfaction and curiosity - the kind of ending that makes your players go, "Wow, what a ride!" and then immediately follow it up with, "But what happens next?" Because if you play your cards right, "next" could be a whole new campaign with new characters, new players, or a world that's been reshaped by the chaos your last group left behind.

Picture this: your old party has faded into legend. Their deeds are now bardic tales, distorted by years of exaggeration and questionable storytelling. New heroes rise, inspired by those stories, eager to carve their own path.

Maybe the new players find artifacts or clues left behind by the old party - a rogue's diary full of half-finished heist plans, a wizard's staff humming with residual magic, or a barbarian's skull-crushing axe embedded in a wall with a note that just says, "Didn't like this wall." These little echoes of the past let you weave continuity into your next campaign without making it feel like a direct sequel.

Who says you even need to stay in the same world? Maybe that epic conclusion sent shockwaves through the very fabric of reality, splintering it into parallel universes where the consequences play out differently. One world might be thriving under the party's legacy of heroism, while another is a post-apocalyptic wasteland because someone thought it'd be fun to mess with that one ominous lever. This way, you get to start fresh while winking at your previous campaign, like an Easter egg only your veteran players will catch.

And if you want to *really* mess with their heads, drop hints that the multiverse isn't just a theory - it's an active problem. Maybe your new party stumbles across dimensional rifts where they catch a brief glimpse of their predecessors, still out there, still adventuring in some other reality.

Imagine the look on your players' faces when they realize their old characters aren't just stories; they're still out there, and their fates are tangled up in this new adventure. It's like running into your ex at the grocery store, except with more magic and fewer awkward conversations about who should keep the ring.

Even if you're switching up everything - new players, new rules, new setting - a well-placed nod to the old campaign can make the whole universe feel alive. Maybe a wise old NPC references "heroes from long ago" who faced a similar threat. Maybe a landmark exists because the old party accidentally blew up the original one. It doesn't have to be big; a subtle nod can make your veteran players feel like they're in on a cosmic joke while your new players just enjoy the ride.

Here's the real secret: the end of one campaign isn't a full stop. It's a semicolon; It's a pause that lets you catch your breath before you launch into the next chaotic chapter. Because no matter how grand the finale, the spirit of the game - the wild creativity, the ridiculous plans, the moments of sheer brilliance and catastrophic failure - doesn't just vanish. It's always waiting, like a plot hook dangling in front of an overly curious rogue.

So, as you wrap things up, leave the door open - just a crack - for the next adventure. Whether it's a direct continuation, a spin-off, or a complete reset with echoes of the past, the end of one story is just the prologue to the next. After all, in the world of TTRPGs, the adventure never really ends. It just takes a snack break.

Now, dear reader, comes my least favorite part of the book, where I beg you to leave me an Amazon review so I am able to keep my lights on. I could go on my usual spiel about "if you enjoyed the book it would mean the world to me if you could leave a review." But this time, instead of spinning you an epic yarn, or offering you a tragic tale, I have a brand new trick up my sleeve. BRIBERY! If you leave a review for my book, hop into the email list as well and respond with a message that you left a review. In return, I will respond with a photo of my cat Schwifty. And I will have to *personally* respond, so you will also get to chat with me directly. But who cares about that, right? The real win here is that photo of Schwifty! He is adorable, and I promise that you will want to see him. "I can just see cats on the internet." You say, slightly annoyed, and while yes, this is true... none of them are Schwifty. I mean, come on, how can you *not* want to see a cat named Schwifty? He's Schwifty! So here are some QR codes to make seeing an adorable cat a bit easier for you. Thank you for reading. I truly appreciate each and every one of you. And enjoy the cat photo.

Leave us a Review!

Join the Email List and Get Your Photo of Schwifty!

Don't forget!

Get your own free copy of the *Advanced RPG Cartography Guide* by scanning the QR code below, joining our mailing list, and unlocking the power to design your own battle maps.

Other Books in the *Advanced RPG Guides* series

Check it out on amazon!

Check it out on amazon!

Made in the USA
Coppell, TX
15 April 2025

48332846R00156